Ghost Stories

GHOST STORIES

SELECTED BY ALEŠ HAMAN AND IRENA ZÍTKOVÁ

ILLUSTRATED BY JAN DUNGEL

Treasure Press

First published in Great Britain in 1987
by Treasure Press
59 Grosvenor Street
London W1

Selected by Aleš Haman and Helena Zítková
Illustrated by Jan Dungel
The texts 'Vera', 'Don Giovanni', 'Dr. Cinderella's Plants' and 'Him?' translated by Stephen Finn
Graphic design by Jiří Schmidt

© 1986 Artia, Prague

ISBN 1 85051 211 6

Printed in Czechoslovakia by Severografia
1/18/08/51-01

Contents

Villiers de l'Isle-Adam
VERA

dedicated to the Countess d'Osmoy

LOVE is stronger than Death, says Solomon; indeed, its mysterious power knows no bounds.

An autumn evening was closing on Paris. A few carriages which had overstayed their hour in the Bois were returning with lighted lamps to the darkened suburb of Saint-Germain. One of them drew up at the entrance to a huge aristocratic residence surrounded by centuries-old gardens. A stone shield topped the arch of the gateway, bearing the coat-of-arms of the ancient family of the Counts d'Athol — a silver star on a blue background, with the motto *'Pallida Victrix'*. The escutcheon was surmounted by a crown trimmed with ermine, over a grand duke's hat.

The heavy doors were flung open, and liveried servants lined up on the steps. They stood there in silence, as still as statues, holding flaming torches above their heads. A man of about thirty or thirty-five, dressed in black, descended from the carriage. His face was deathly pale. With bowed head and somehow soulless mien, the Count d'Athol slowly ascended the steps of his historic residence and went inside.

With a halting, listless gait the count mounted the white staircase which led to the chamber where, that very morning, he had laid her on a bed of violets in her velvet-lined coffin. Vera — his joy, his despair, his bride, now departed, shrouded in white batiste.

The chamber door opened soundlessly; he pushed aside the heavy curtain and stepped inside.

Everything was still lying where she had left it the day before. Sudden death had snatched her from his arms, drawn its cold fingers across her lips. She scarcely had time to kiss her dear Roger goodbye, silently and with a last smile, before her long eyelashes closed like shrouds over those soft, dark eyes.

The dire day had passed. When the agonizing ceremony in the family tomb was over, the Count d'Athol had taken his leave of the mourners right there in the cemetery. He was left alone. For a few moments he gazed vacantly into space; then, taking a hold of himself, he went back down into the awesome crypt where his loved one lay between cold marble walls. He closed the wrought-iron gate behind him. There was incense smouldering in a tripod in front of the coffin; behind the head of the departed was a crown-shaped cluster of lamps, whose flickering light threw myriad tiny stars across her face.

There he remained for the rest of the day, rooted to the spot and steeped in memories, moved by that unique mixture of tenderness and despair. It was almost six, and dusk was falling, when he finally left her shrine. He locked the tomb and drew the silver key from the lock; then, as

An autumn evening was closing on Paris.

he stood on the bottom step, he turned and tossed it gently through the bars of the gate. Why? Perhaps on account of a sudden, inexplicable resolution never to return.

Now here he was, back in this chamber of bereavement.

The window, framed by its mauve cashmere curtains interwoven with gold, was open. A last ray of evening light fell upon the large portrait of the deceased in its time-seasoned wooden frame. The count looked around him, taking in the whole sad scene: the robe, lying across the armchair where she had flung it the night before; on the mantelpiece her jewels, a pearl necklace; over there a half-open fan, and the crystal bottles with the perfumes her skin would exhale no more. The bed, with its whorled ebony posts, was still unmade. Beside the pillow, which still held the print where her adorable head had lain amid the lace, he saw a handkerchief sprinkled with drops of blood, where for an instant her young soul had caught its wings. The open piano seemed to hold the echo of an unfinished melody. The Indian flowers she had picked in the hothouse were now withering in the antique Saxe vases. On the black fur rug beside one of the bed-legs lay the tiny slippers of oriental velvet, with Vera's frivolous motto picked out in tiny pearls: *Qui verra Véra l'aimera.* Only yesterday morning his loved one's feet had tripped back and forth in them, caressed at every step by the swansdown with which they were trimmed! And over in the shadows stood the pendulum clock, whose spring he had broken so it could strike the hours no more.

She was gone, then! But where to? Was he to go on living? What was the sense in that? It was impossible, absurd.

The count became lost in memories. He recalled exactly how it had been. It was six months since their wedding. It was at some embassy ball they had first met...yes, he could remember the moment quite distinctly. He could see her standing there, radiant. Their eyes had met; they had seen each other's souls, knew they were kindred spirits. They must love each other for ever.

The malicious gossip, the knowing smiles, the insinuations – all those obstacles people set up to delay the inevitable happiness of those who belong to each other – all evaporated before the perfect faith they had in each other from the start.

Vera, tired of the empty ceremonies of the company, had made use of the first pretext that offered itself to approach him, dispensing in a sublime gesture with the banal courtesies which erode the precious minutes of our lives.

Oh! At the very first words they exchanged, the meaningless preoccupations of their insipid companions were as the flight of night birds, returning to the shadows! What smiles they gave each other! How blissfully they embraced!

But there was indeed something out of the ordinary in the nature these two shared. That belief in the supernatural which most mortals seemed to hold stirred in them no more than a vague astonishment. For them matters of the spirit were a closed book, something with which they did not concern themselves, which they neither defended nor denied. So, recognizing that the outside world was alien to them, as soon as they were married they rejected it, to live in isolation in this sombre old mansion, where the barrier of the gardens deadened all sound from outside.

There the two lovers had engrossed themselves in their love, had become so intoxicated by it that for them it was the only reality. Then, suddenly, the spell was broken. A cruel misfortune had torn them apart.

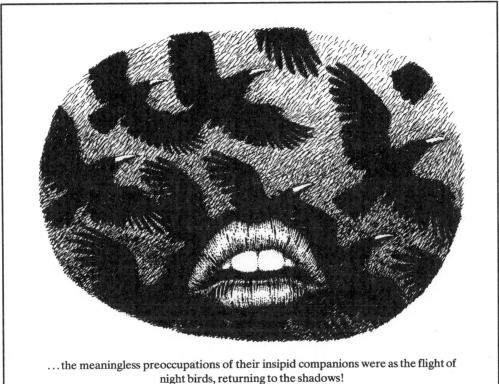

. . . the meaningless preoccupations of their insipid companions were as the flight of night birds, returning to the shadows!

What dark shadow had snatched away his dearest? Dead? But why dead? Does the soul leave a violin with the shriek of a snapping string?

The hours went by.

Through the window he watched darkness overtake the heavens. Night seemed to take on a personality — a queen, making her melancholy way into exile. Only the diamond brooch which adorned her cloak of mourning — Venus — shone over the treetops, alone against the blue-black sky.

'It's Vera,' he whispered.

At the sound of that name, spoken almost silently, he shivered, as if awaking from a dream. Then he turned and surveyed the room once more.

The objects in the room were now illuminated by a glow which had until now been scarcely perceptible, that of a night-light, which imbued the shadows with a bluish tinge, and which the darkness that had slid across the firmament now marked out like another star. It was the incense-breathing night-light which burned in front of the old triptych, an heirloom of Vera's family. Framed in mellowed, precious wood, it hung between the mirror and her portrait. The flickering light was picked up by the necklace, lying on the mantlepiece along with the other jewels.

The halo of the Madonna in her heavenly robes took on a rosy hue from the Byzantine cross, whose fine red outline, melting in the reflection, gave a crimson tint to the illuminated pearls. Since her childhood, Vera's large eyes had always held a fascination for the motherly face of the family Madonna. Her nature, alas! would allow her no more than a *superstitious* love for the Blessed Virgin, and this she offered from time to time – naively, pensively – as she passed in front of the light.

At the sight of it, the count, touched to his inmost soul by painful memories, strode forward and blew out the flame. Then, reaching out in the dark, he sounded the bell.

An old servant, dressed in black, appeared at the door. He was holding a lamp, which he set down in front of the countess's portrait. When he turned to face the count again, he felt a chill of superstitious horror to see his master smiling, as though nothing had happened.

'Raymond,' said the count, calmly, 'the countess and I are terribly tired this evening: you will serve supper at ten. And, Raymond, we have decided to live here in complete solitude from tomorrow. None of the servants except yourself is to stay here another night. Pay them three years' wages and release them at once. Then you will draw the bolts and light all the candelabra in the dining room. Your services will suffice – we shall not be receiving any more visitors.'

The old man trembled, studying his master attentively. The count lit a cigar and went down into the gardens.

At first the servant thought that profound, desperate grief had driven his master crazy. He had known the count since boyhood, and he knew at once that the shock of too sudden a return to reality might prove fatal. On no account must he betray the pretence.

He hung his head. Was he to play the role of a devoted accomplice in

V. de l'Isle-Adam

this crazy dream? To obey? To go on waiting on *them,* in defiance of the fact of death? What a strange idea! Who knew whether it would survive the night. Tomorrow, tomorrow — alas! what might tomorrow bring? But it was his sacred duty. What right had he to question it?

Leaving the room, the servant went and carried out the count's orders to the letter. That night saw the beginning of a strange new way of life.

It was necessary to create a weird illusion.

The initial awkwardness soon wore off. Raymond played his part uneasily at first, but respect and tenderness for his master led him to create a role so natural that within three weeks there were times when he would be deceived for a moment by his own good will. He tried not to think about it, but he was sometimes seized with a sort of vertigo, feeling the need to remind himself that the countess was really dead. He was getting caught up in the macabre game, and frequently lost touch with reality. Soon it was no simple matter to convince himself that it was a game, to take stock of his own thoughts. He realized that by and by he was sure to submit himself entirely to the awesome spell the count was casting all around them. He began to feel a quiet, indeterminate fear.

D'Athol, indeed, lived in complete unawareness of his beloved wife's death. It was inevitable that he should feel her presence everywhere, so fully had the young woman's being become blended with his own. He would sit on a bench out in the garden on a sunny day, reading out loud the poetry she loved best; then he would sit by the fireside of an evening, with two cups of tea on the table, chatting with the smiling illusion seated opposite him in the armchair.

Days, nights and weeks passed. Neither of them knew what they were doing. Such strange things were happening now that it was becoming difficult to make out where exactly imagination and reality coincided. There was a presence floating in the air, a form trying to become visible, to materialize.

D'Athol lived a double life, in a state of heightened perception. There would be a soft, pale face, glimpsed between blinks of the eye, like the after-image of a bright light; a sudden, gentle chord sounded on the piano; a kiss which closed his lips as he was about to speak. A woman's response would be awakened in him to the things he had said, such a doubling of his self that he would sense, like a rolling mist, the stupefyingly sweet perfume of his dearest as it drifted past him. At night, half way between wakefulness and sleep, he would hear softly spoken words. He perceived all this. Death's power had been challenged by some unknown force!

Once, he felt and saw her so clearly that he tried to touch her, but the movement caused her to dissolve.

'My child!' he murmured, with a smile.

When her name-day came round, he light-heartedly slipped an everlasting flower in the bouquet he laid on her pillow.

'That's because she thinks she's dead,' he said.

Thanks to the unshaking and all-powerful resolution with which the

A glimpse of a black velvet gown beyond a turn in the walk...

Count d'Athol's love recreated the life and presence of his wife inside the solitary mansion, in the end the way of life there took on a certain sombre and persuasive charm. Not even Raymond had any misgivings now, for he had grown accustomed to the existence.

A glimpse of a black velvet gown beyond a turn in the walk; a laughing voice calling him into the salon; the tinkle of a bell that roused him in the morning like before — all this was now familiar. He was sure that his dead mistress was playing a child's game of hide-and-seek with him; but then it was only natural, when she felt so well loved.

A year went by.

On the day of the anniversary, the count, sitting in front of the fire in Vera's room, had just finished reading her a Florentine *fabliau*. Closing the book and reaching for the teapot, he said:

'*Douschka,* do you remember the Vallée-des-Roses on the banks of the Lahn? The Quatre-Tours chateau? Doesn't the story remind you of it?'

He stood up, surveying himself in the blue-tinted mirror. He seemed paler than usual. He picked up a pearl bracelet lying in a bowl, and peered closely at the pearls. Hadn't Vera just slipped it off her hand, before undressing? The pearls were still warm, their sheen softened, as if by the heat of her body. And the opal in her Siberian necklace would always grow dull, as though pining, if the young woman ignored it for any length of time. Didn't Vera love it for its fidelity? That evening the stone shone as if it had just been laid aside, as if her rare magnetism pervaded it still. As he replaced the necklace with its precious stone, he happened to touch the batiste handkerchief, on which the drops of blood were as fresh and scarlet as carnations in the snow! Who had turned over the last page of music on the piano? What was that − the night-light in front of the triptych had relit itself! Yes, its golden flame threw a mystical light on the face of the Madonna, with its closed eyes! And those freshly-picked oriental flowers blossoming in the old Saxe vases − whose hand had placed them there? The room seemed more joyful than usual, endowed with more life. But nothing could surprise the count; it all seemed so utterly normal to him that he paid no heed even when the pendulum clock, whose spring he had snapped in that first moment of bitterness a year before, suddenly struck the hour.

But that evening it really did seem as if Vera was striving to return from the shadowy depths, to re-enter that room which was so imbued with her. She had left there so much of herself! All that had epitomized her existence was drawing her there. Her charm filled the air: surely the passionate strength of will shown by her husband might loosen the bonds of invisibility which tied her!

She was a necessity there; everything she had loved was there.

She surely longed to come and smile again in the mysterious mirror where she had so often admired her lily-white face. His dearest must have trembled amidst her violets, there beneath the lifeless lamps; she must have shivered, alone in the tomb, to see the silver key cast onto the flags. She, too, wanted to come to him! But her will was dissipating itself in the domain of incense and isolation. Death is final only for those who hope in heaven; but was not death, and heaven, and life for her no more or less than their love? His unreturned kiss called her lips from the shadows. The melodies of the past, the heady words once exchanged, the garments she had worn and which still retained her perfume, the magical jewels which pined for her in some mysterious way – and above all the immense and absolute impression of her presence, shared by everything in the room, all had long since been calling her, drawing her gradually back again, so that all that remained was for Vera herself to appear, released from the sleep of death!

Ah! but ideas have a life of their own... The count traced the form of his loved one in the air, and knew that the void had to be filled by the one being compatible with his own – or the universe would crumble. At that moment he sensed, finally, simply and absolutely, that she was there, in the room. Of that he had the same complacent certainty as he had of his own existence, and everything in the room was permeated with the same conviction. He could see her there! And since the only thing lacking was Vera herself, tangibly, externally, she had to be there; the great dream of life and death must for a moment open a little its infinite gates! Faith had paved the way of resurrection for her! A fresh peal of laughter brought the chamber to life. The count turned round: there, before his eyes, born of sheer willpower and remembrance, leaning lightly on the lace pillow with her hand in her raven locks and a delicious smile on her lips, was Vera. She was as beautiful as ever, and her big eyes were still hazy with sleep.

'Roger!' she said, in a faraway voice.

He stepped forward, and their lips met with a joy that was divine, oblivious, immortal.

Now they realized that they really were a single being.

The hours slipped by unmarked, in this first ecstatic mingling of heaven and earth. But suddenly the count shuddered, as if struck by a fatal recollection.

'Ah! Now I remember!' he gasped. 'What is the matter with me? Why, you are dead!'

As he spoke the last word, the mysterious flame which burned before the triptych went out. The pale forelight of dawn – a banal, dismal, rainswept dawn – filtered into the room through the lace curtains. The candles faded and died, an acrid smoke rising from their smouldering wicks. The fire in the hearth choked beneath a layer of ashes; the flowers withered and dropped in a matter of moments, and the pendulum of the clock slowly came to rest. The certitude which had pervaded everything had suddenly slipped away. The opal had lost its sheen, and lay there lifeless again. The drops of blood on the white handkerchief had faded. And the pale, ardent vision slid from the desperate arms which tried to embrace it once more, dissolved into air, and was gone. A faint sigh of adieu, distant but quite distinct, reached down to his very soul. The count rose, realizing he was alone. His dream was gone in an instant. A single word had snapped the

Suddenly, as if in answer, a shiny object fell from the bed onto the black fur rug...

magnetic thread of which its radiant fabric was woven. Now a sense of death prevailed.

Just as the little glass tears which in disordered aggregation will withstand a hammer blow, but at a gentle tap on their needle-fine tip are reduced to a soft powder, all that had been vanished.

'Oh!' he murmured. 'It is the end! She is lost! Alone again! How am I to reach you now? Show me the way to you!'

Suddenly, as if in answer, a shiny object fell from the bed onto the black fur rug, making a metallic thud. A ray of light from the dreadful, earthly dawn glinted upon it. The abandoned lover bent to pick it up, and his face lit up with a sublime smile: it was the key to the family tomb.

Ernst Theodor Amadeus Hoffmann
DON GIOVANNI

A Strange Adventure that Befell
a Certain Devotee on his Travels

THE sound of a bell and a loud shout of 'Take your seats, please!' roused me from my peaceful doze. There was a droning of double-basses, a rumble of drums, a hooting of trumpets; an oboe held a steady A, and violins were tuned. I rubbed my eyes: could the devil be up to his tricks again? But no,

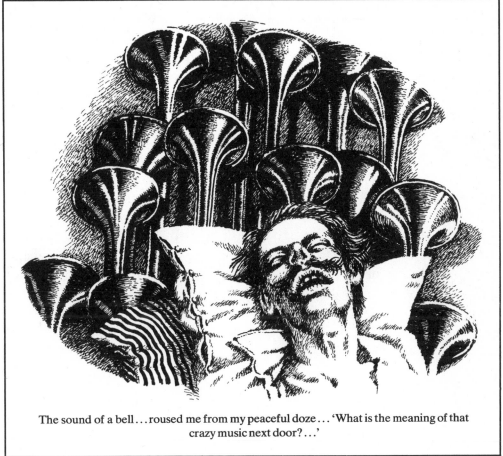

The sound of a bell...roused me from my peaceful doze...'What is the meaning of that crazy music next door?...'

I was there in the hotel room I had taken the night before, quite exhausted from my long journey. Hanging in front of my nose was the generous tassel of a bell-pull. I gave a sharp tug, and a waiter entered.

'What is the meaning of that crazy music next door? Are you by any chance holding a concert in the hotel?'

'Your Excellency,' – (I had drunk champagne with my lunch) – 'Your Excellency, I daresay, has not yet heard that our hotel is connected with a theatre. That padded door opens onto a corridor leading to number twenty-three – the guest box.'

'Theatre? Guest box?'

'Indeed: a small box for two or three people, reserved for honoured guests. It has green upholstery and grilles on the windows, and it looks straight down onto the stage. If it please Your Excellency, today's performance is the opera *Don Giovanni* by the famous Herr Mozart of Vienna. The price is one thaler eight groschen, which will be added to your bill.'

The waiter was already opening the door of the box as he spoke these last words, so rapidly had I entered the small corridor at the words *Don Giovanni*. The auditorium was a roomy one for so relatively modest a town; it was tastefully furnished, and the lighting was superb. The boxes and stalls were packed. The opening chords of the overture had been enough to assure me that the orchestra was an excellent one, and should the singers prove to be of some merit at least, the performance of this masterpiece promised to be a most gratifying one.

During the *andante* I was seized with a horror of the underworld *regno al pianto*:[1] a chilling foreboding of something terrible gripped my heart. The exultant fanfare in the seventh bar of the *allegro* came like an ill-timed and irreverent whoop of joy; I could see the fiery demons from the depths of darkness reaching out their searing claws to where carefree mortals gaily danced, treading the thin crust of a bottomless chasm. In my mind's eye I could clearly perceive a struggle between human nature and the awful, nameless powers that weave their webs around a man and wait for him to fall to his doom. At last, the storm of sound subsided, as the curtain went up.

Frowning and shivering, wrapped in a cloak, Leporello strode in front of the façade which formed the centrepiece of the set. *'Notte e giorno faticar…'*[2] So it was to be in Italian! Italian, in this provincial town in Germany? *Ah che piacere!*[3] Then I was to hear the recitatives, everything, just as the great maestro had conceived it! Now Don Giovanni himself comes running out of the house, followed by Donna Anna, tugging at the villain's cloak. What a figure of a woman! Perhaps she might have been a trifle taller, a little slimmer. Maybe her movements on stage were somewhat lacking in majesty. But that head and face! Eyes radiating sparks

1) *regno al pianto* – 'realm of tears', i. e. hell.
2) *'Notte e giorno faticar…'* – he's at it day and night.
3) *Ah che piacere* – what a pleasure.

of love, anger, hatred and despair that, slakeless as Greek fire, burn their way into your soul! Loosened plaits of dark hair tumble down her temples in a flood of ringlets. And that voice! *'Non sperar se non m'uccidi...'*[4] Through the storm of the instruments, like fiery lightning flashes, stab notes that are wrought of ethereal metal. Don Giovanni tries in vain to tear himself away. Does he really want to? Why does he not thrust the woman from him with his powerful fist and make his escape? Is he paralysed by his evil deed, or is

It suggests the hypnotic magic of a rattlesnake, as though any woman who looked at him would be unable to forget him...

his courage drained by the conflict of love and hate raging within him? The old father has paid with his life for his foolishness in taking on a strong adversary in the dark; Don Giovanni and Leporello step forward onto the proscenium in an exchange of recitative. Don Giovanni has doffed his cloak and stands there resplendent in fine scarlet velvet embroidered with silver. He is a fine, massive figure of a man, with a face of masculine beauty, an

4) *'Non sperar se non m'uccidi...'* − do not hope, lest you kill me.

aristocratic nose, penetrating eyes, softly moulded lips. The peculiar way
the muscles of his forehead pucker the eyebrows sometimes lends his face
a Mephistophelean touch, in no way detracting from its handsomeness, but
sending an involuntary shiver up the onlooker's spine. It suggests the
hypnotic magic of a rattlesnake, as though any woman who looked at him
would be unable to forget him and, driven by some mysterious force, would
be compelled to seal her own fate. The tall, gaunt Leporello shuffles up and
down beside his master in his red and white striped tunic, red cloak and
white hat topped with a scarlet feather. His face conveys a strange mixture
of benevolence and villainy, of fastidiousness and mocking insolence. His
black eyebrows stand out weirdly against the grey hair and beard. The old
rogue seems the perfect servant and accomplice for Don Giovanni.

The pair have escaped safely over the wall. Torches are brought, and
Donna Anna enters with Don Ottavio, a petty and foppish youth of not
more than about twenty-one. As Donna Anna's fiancé he must have been
a guest in the house, that they were able to summon him so promptly; he
might have rushed to her father's rescue at the very first sounds of
a struggle, which he must surely have heard. But then he would have to
make his toilet first, and in any case he probably wasn't too anxious to
venture out at night. '*Ma qual mai s'offre, o dei, spettacolo funesto agli occhi
miei!*'[5] The terrible, heart-rending notes of this recitative and duet convey
more than mere despair over the commission of a heinous crime. The words
are wrenched from a heart which has not only been weighed down by the
tragedy of Don Giovanni's poorly-matched duel with her father. Such
dejection as this can only be the product of a vicious, deadly struggle within
one's own breast.

Tall, thin Donna Elvira, still bearing the traces of a beauty that must
have been considerable, had just chided Don Giovanni for his treachery
— *Tu nido d'inganni*"[6] — and the compassionate Leporello had commented
quite aptly '*parla come un libro stampato*'[7], when I suddenly had the feeling
someone was sitting in the box behind me or beside me. It would have been
no problem to open the door and slip silently inside. The awareness came
like a stab to the heart! How glad I had been to be in the box alone! I had
looked forward to an uninterrupted appreciation of this superb rendering of
an operatic masterpiece, hoped to take hold of it with every nerve in my
body, like an octopus gripping its prey, to suck it dry of emotional
nourishment. A single word, which might be a foolish one at that, would
suffice to break the beautiful spell of that wonderful poetry and music.

5) '*Ma qual…*' etc. – O God, what a mournful scene meets my eyes!
6) '*Tu nido d'inganni*' – you nest of deception.
7) '*parla come un libro stampato*' – she speaks like a printed book.

E.T.A. Hoffmann

I resolved to take no notice at all of my companion, to remain entirely engrossed in the performance, neither speaking nor turning to face him. Resting my head on my hand, with my back to my neighbour, I kept my eyes fixed on the stage.

The opera progressed along the same lines as its excellent opening. The diminutive, fastidious and lovesick Zerlina sang her charming little song to soothe Masetto, the kindhearted fool. In the wild aria *'Fin ch'han dal vino'*[8] Don Giovanni openly revealed his derangement, his contempt for the insignificant creatures who surrounded him, placed there solely for his amusement, that he might malignantly interfere in their worthless toing and froing. The muscles of his forehead worked more vigorously than ever. Enter masked singers, whose tercet is a prayer that rises to heaven like a clear ray of light. The backdrop rises to reveal a scene of frenzied merriment: amid the chink of goblets the peasants and masked guests at Don Giovanni's banquet carouse noisily. Now, bound by an irrevocable oath, the three avengers arrive on the scene. At once all is more festive than ever — until the dance begins. Zerlina is saved, and in the thundrous finale Don Giovanni boldly faces his adversaries with drawn sword. Wrenching from the bridegroom's hand his splendid dagger, the anti-hero hacks his way to freedom, laying his attackers low like Roland the army of the tyrant Cymorque, until they are all piled up in a quite amusing fashion.

It had already seemed to me more than once that I could feel behind me a gentle, warm breathing, could hear the rustle of silk. I suspected that there was a woman in the box with me, but, immersed in a world of poetry provided by the opera, I took no heed of the fact. Now that the curtain had fallen, I glanced at my companion for the first time. Words cannot express my amazement: behind me stood Donna Anna, dressed in the same clothes as those she wore on stage, where I had seen her a short while ago, and fixing me with the penetrating gaze of those soulful eyes.

I stared at her, speechless. Her mouth (or so it seemed to me) was drawn into a light, ironic smile, in which I could see my own lamentable figure as in a mirror. I felt an obligation to address her, but my tongue, paralysed with wonder — I might almost say fright — refused to cooperate. At last, at long last I managed to say, almost breathlessly: 'How do you come to be here?' She replied at once, in pure Tuscan, that if I were unable to understand and speak Italian, she would have to forego the pleasure of conversation with me, since she knew no other tongue. Her sweet words had the quality of song. Her deep blue eyes were more striking than ever

---

8) *'Fin ch'han dal vino'* — as long as the wine flows.

when she spoke, and at each flash from them my heart was stabbed with fire, so that my veins pulsed wildly and my nerves began to vibrate. That it was Donna Anna, there was not the slightest doubt. I did not stop to consider how it was possible for her to be on stage and here in the box with me, both at the same time. Just as a blissful dream may link the incompatible, or as faith in the supernatural comprehends the incomprehensible, places it with unfaltering assurance alongside the so-called natural phenomena of life, so I, in the proximity of this enchanting woman, fell into a sort of somnambulance, where it was quite clear to me that we were joined so closely by some mysterious affinity that she was unable to leave my side even when she was on stage.

How I should like, dear Theodore, to repeat to you word for word the remarkable conversation which unfolded between the signora and me. But the moment I try to write down in German the things she said, it seems so stiff and lacklustre, and every sentence seems far too clumsy to express what she said in Tuscan with such ease and elegance.

When she spoke of Don Giovanni, of her role, it was as if the whole masterpiece were revealed to me for the first time in all its profundity; everything became clear to me – I had a distinct view of the fantastic visions of a strange world, just as if it had been my own. She said that music was her whole life, that when she was singing it often seemed to her that she understood many things that were hidden deep inside her, things that could not be expressed in mere words. 'Yes, I understand,' she went on, her eyes ablaze and her voice rising, 'but all around me there is only a cold lifelessness. When they applaud the difficult passages, the theatrical effects, it is as though an icy hand were grasping my burning heart! But *you* understand me: I know that you, too, have in front of you that beautiful, romantic realm ruled by the divine magic of music!'

'How... most wonderful of women, do you know me?'

'Was it not your heart that poured forth the enchanted ravings of an endlessly unrequited love, through the mouth of the unfortunate heroine in your last opera? I have understood you – your soul has been opened up to me in song! Yes,' (here she addressed me by name) 'I have sung you, just as I *am* all your music.'

A bell announced the end of the interval; Donna Anna's face, quite without make-up, took on a sudden pallor. Her hand went to her heart, as if she felt some sharp pain. 'Poor Anna – your most terrible moment is coming,' she said, softly, and she vanished from the box.

The first act had enthralled me, but now, after such a strange experience, the music had a quite different, a peculiar effect on me. It was as though I had achieved the fulfilment, long promised, of the most beautiful dreams of another world, as if the notes were enchanted with the fleeting intimations of an inflamed soul and now, through some magic, had to take on the form of remarkable recognition. During the scene with Donna Anna I felt my whole being vibrate with blissful intoxication, as if I were brushed by some delightful, warm breeze. Involuntarily, I closed my eyes, and a burning kiss seemed to sear my lips; but that kiss was a note of music, lingering oh! so long in unquenchable longing.

The finale began with irreverent gaiety: *'Gia la mensa è preparata!'* [9] Don Giovanni was sitting there, embracing a different girl with each arm and opening one bottle after another, submitting to the spirits of the wine, which came bubbling out of it after their long imprisonment. The room where he sat was of no great size, and at the back of it a broad Gothic window looked out onto the night. Even as Elvira began to remind the faithless Don Giovanni of all his promises, the lightning flashes and subdued rumbling of an approaching storm were frequently apparent. At last there came a mighty banging at the door. Elvira and the four girls ran away, and amid the awe-inspiring chords of the kingdom of the damned a gigantic marble statue appeared, dwarfing Don Giovanni to insignificance. The ground shook beneath the thunderous steps of the colossus. Through the din of the storm and the whine of demons Don Giovanni calls out his fearful: No! The hour of his doom has come. The statue vanishes. Thick smoke fills the room, and out of it step fearsome monsters. Here and there amid the devils we catch sight of Don Giovanni writhing in the torments of hell. There is a roar like a thousand claps of thunder, and both Don Giovanni and the demons have disappeared in some mysterious way. Leporello is lying senseless in a corner of the room. There is a sense of relief as others enter and search in vain for Don Giovanni, whom the powers of the underworld have snatched from the reach of earthly vengeance. It is only then that one has the feeling he has himself escaped the fiends of hell.

Now Donna Anna enters, quite altered. Her cheeks are deathly pale, her eyes dull, her voice wavers and falters. But it is this which lends powerful emotion to the *duettino* with her delicate fiancé who, now that the heavens have relieved him of the perilous role of avenger, wants to get married at once.

9) *'Gia la mensa è preparata'* – the food is ready.

The choral fugue brought the whole work to a magnificent close, and in a mood of elation I hurried back to my room. The waiter invited me to take supper downstairs, and I followed him mechanically.

There was an annual fair in the town, so that an élite company had gathered at table. The topic of conversation was today's performance of *Don Giovanni*. On the whole they praised the Italians and their captivating opera, but their minor reservations, which at times seemed even waggish,

Thick smoke fills the room, and out of it step fearsome monsters.

showed that none of them understood the profound significance of this opera of operas. Don Ottavio had impressed them greatly. To one member of the company Donna Anna had seemed too passionate. He explained that on stage it was essential to observe moderation, to avoid any excessively importunate expression of feeling. The account of the attack had left him in complete consternation. The gentleman in question took a pinch of snuff, and looked at his neighbour with an expression of indescribable foolishness as the latter gave his own opinion of the prima donna. When all was said and done, he opined, the Italian woman was a very beautiful lady, only she paid too little attention to her dress and outward appearance. In the very scene they had been talking about her coiffure had come loose and covered her whole face in demiprofile! Then someone began quietly to sing *'Fin ch'han dal vino'*, and one lady commented that it had been Don Giovanni himself whom she had liked least of all. The Italian frowned too much, was too serious, and failed to imbue this frivolous and flighty character with an adequate degree of levity. They had high praise for the fall into hell in the last act. Sick of their prattle, I hurriedly retired to my room.

In Box Number Twenty-three

How disquieted, how fretful I felt in that stuffy room! At midnight, I fancied I heard your voice, dear Theodore! You spoke my name distinctly, and there was a rustling sound over by the padded door. Why should I not return to the scene of my strange adventure? Perhaps I should see both you and her, she who filled my soul to the brim. Nothing could be simpler than to take the table there, along with a couple of candles and my writing materials. The waiter comes looking for me with a glass of punch; the room is empty, the padded door open wide. He comes after me into the box and shakes his head. I tell him to set down the glass and leave me, but on his way out he glances at me again — itching to ask an inquisitive question. I turn my back on him, lean over the edge of the box and look down on the deserted stage. In a series of strange glintings thrown by the magic light of my candles, its outlines loom out of the darkness in an altered, fairytale configuration. A draught passes through the theatre, lightly shifting the stage curtain. What if it were to rise? What if Donna Anna were to appear, pursued by fearful apparitions? 'Donna Anna!' I call involuntarily. The sound of my voice dies away in the emptiness, but down in the orchestra the souls of the instruments stir — a strange tone floats quiveringly upwards, and it is as if that dear name were echoed in it! I cannot resist shivering, but it sends a pleasant vibration through my nerves.

I have overcome my melancholy now, and I should like, my dear Theodore, to give you at least an inkling of how I now understand — as I suppose for the first time properly — the profound sense of the magnificent work of that divine master. Only a poet can understand a poet;

only a romantic spirit may penetrate a romantic work, only a poetically inspired soul that has been initiated in the holy of holies can comprehend that which is spoken by another initiate in creative ecstasy.

If we do not perceive in the poem, in *Don Giovanni,* a deeper significance, if we are aware only of the external action, we can scarcely hope to understand how Mozart was able to invent and enshrine in poetry music such as that. A worldly fellow who sets too great a store by wine and women arrogantly invites to his feast the stone statue of an old father he stabbed to death in self-defence. Truly, there is nothing especially poetic about that, and to tell the truth a fellow like him does not deserve the honour of a private viewing of hell such as was afforded him. For his benefit alone the stone figure, brought to life by a soul that had already passed the pearly gates, took the trouble of coming down off his horse and urging him to repent at the eleventh hour, and the Prince of Darkness sent the cream of his demons to escort the sinner personally back to his kingdom with a great firework display.

Let me tell you, Theodore: Don Giovanni was endowed by nature, as the best-loved of her children, with all that brings a mortal closer to divinity, all that raises him above the vulgar mob, above the mass-produced creatures that nature churns out in her workshops like a row of zeroes, so that you have to put some number in front of them for them to have any value at all. What was it that marked him out to be a victor, a ruler? His strong, exquisite body; education, which fell upon his heart like a glowing spark, igniting in it a notion of the highest goals; profound feeling, a sharp intellect. But the terrible consequence of original sin is that the dark one has been able to come close to a man, to set artful traps for him even in that which is an expression of his divine nature, his effort to achieve the highest goals. It is this conflict between the powers of heaven and hell that gives rise to the notion of human life, just as victory in it gives rise to the notion of life everlasting.

Don Giovanni was intoxicated by the idea that because of his physical and mental superiority he could assume power over life and death, and an ever-burning desire which caused the blood to course hotly in his veins drove him to grasp, greedily and incessantly, all that this world can offer, vainly seeking satiety. There is perhaps nothing in the world that can elevate a man in his true essence to greater heights than love. This mystic and powerful force destroys and refines the most spiritual elements of mortal existence. Small wonder, then, that Don Giovanni hoped to quench in love the yearning which ravaged his breast, and that it was here that the devil slipped the noose around his neck. The dark one's cunning sowed in Don Giovanni's soul the idea that love can fulfil, here on earth, that celestial promise which lies hidden in our hearts, the longing for eternity, that which links us with the supernatural. Don Giovanni hurried from one woman to the next, always thinking that he had again failed to find the right one, always hoping to fulfil his ideal. In the end the whole of life on earth must

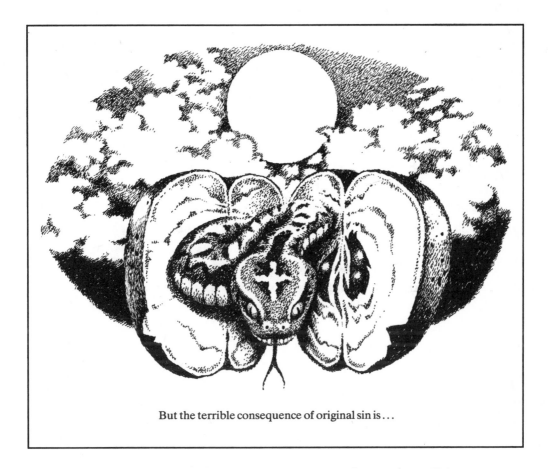

But the terrible consequence of original sin is ...

seem to him flat and colourless, and in his disdain for mankind he turns against that which once seemed to him the height of human existence, and which has so bitterly disappointed him. His total rejection of the ordinary notion of life, which he considers himself to be above, and the bitter sneer he directs towards those who still seek in true love and its foundation in society at least a hint of the fulfilment of those higher yearnings sown in our breast by hostile nature, lead him to launch an attack on such relationships wherever he finds them. He leaves behind him a trail of destruction, arrogantly defying the unknown force that governs our fate, seeming to him as it does to be a malignant monster, which plays a cruel game with the creations of its malicious whims. Every time he seduces a beloved bride, destroys the happiness of lovers with a wound that will never heal, he sees it as a new and glorious triumph over that hostile power, and each new victory raises him higher above life, where there is no room to spread his wings, above nature, above the Creator! So it is that he does indeed climb higher and higher above life, but only to come crashing down into hell. The seduction of Donna Anna and all it entails is the peak of his achievement.

Donna Anna is as generously endowed by nature as Don Giovanni himself. Just as he was once an enormously strong, handsome man, so is she an exquisitely beautiful woman with a pure soul, over which the devil has no power. All the black arts of hell can do no more than wreak her earthly ruin. As soon as Satan has consummated this work of destruction, the heavens decree that the hounds of hell shall accomplish vengeance. Don Giovanni vauntingly invites the statue of the dead father to his dissolute revels. The father's soul, lifted up to heaven, recognizes for the first time the identity of this sinner, takes pity on him, and does not hesitate to take on a terrible form in order to bring him to repentance. But Don Giovanni's heart is already so corrupted, so hardened, that not even the promise of celestial bliss can awaken hope in it, turn it to the paths of righteousness.

You will surely have noticed, my dear Theodore, that I spoke of Donna Anna's seduction. I will explain to you briefly, and as best I can at this moment, when ideas and thoughts are pouring from the depths of my heart faster than words can express them, how I see the relation of these two conflicting personalities, Don Giovanni and Donna Anna, in the music, without regard to the text.

I have already said that Donna Anna stands in opposition to Don Giovanni. But supposing it had been her fate to reveal to him, in that very love which was, by Satan's design, to lead to her downfall, the divine substance with which he was endowed, thus rescuing him from the despair of vain seeking? He met her too late, when he was already enslaved by evil, so that only a demonic urge to destroy her could overcome him. Nor was she spared! When he fled the house, the deed had already been accomplished. Hell fire had eaten into her heart, making all resistance vain. Only he, Don Giovanni, was able to kindle in her such passion, only he, himself inflamed as only a child of hell can be. When, having done the deed, he sought to flee, then the consciousness of ruin overwhelmed her, tormented her, like a terrible monster, spitting venom and dealing death. Consciousness that Don Giovanni has killed her father, that she is betrothed to the cold, effeminate, trivial Don Ottavio, whom she once thought she loved; then, in the depths of her soul there is the consuming fire of what was once love, now turned to hate. All this is rending her heart. She feels that only Don Giovanni's destruction can bring peace to a soul tormented by mortal agony. But this peace at the same time means her death. Thus she constantly calls upon her frosty fiancé to avenge her; she pursues the deceiver herself, and only when the powers of darkness drag him off to hell does she calm down a little. Still, she cannot reconcile herself with the wishes of her impatient bridegroom: *'Lascia, o caro, un anno ancora, allo sfogo del mio cor!'*[10] She does not live that year out: Don Ottavio never embraces the woman whom only her piety saved from becoming a bride of Satan.

How vividly I felt all this in the depths of my soul at the resounding chords of the first recitative and the account of the nocturnal attack! Even the scene in the second act − *'Crudele...'*[11] − where at first sight Donna Anna speaks only of Don Ottavio, reveals in a series of covert implications the inner situation of a soul for which all earthly happiness is lost. What, then, is the meaning of that truly strange addition, which the poet must surely have made without deliberation: *'Forse un giorno il cielo ancora sentirà pietà di me!'*?[12]

A clock strikes two! I feel a hot, electric breeze, the light scent of the fine Italian perfume that betrayed my companion's presence in the evening. I am overcome by a blissful feeling I could only express in music. The draught in the theatre grows stronger, until the strings of the piano begin to sound softly; Lord! I could swear I hear from afar, on the wings of sound spread by some ethereal orchestra, Donna Anna's voice: *'Non me dir bel, idol mio!'*[13] An unknown, distant realm of spirits opens up to me − O fabulously beautiful land of the jinn, where both unspeakable pain and indescribable joy fill to the brim the cup of earthly desire! Allow me to enter the circle of your enchanting visions! Would that the dream you have sent as a messenger, sometimes of joy, sometimes of sorrow, might, when sleep locks the body in leaden chains, lead my spirit to your meadows beyond the clouds!

10) *'Lascia...'* etc. − give me another year so that my heart may speak.
11) *'Crudele...'* − cruel.
12) *'Forse...'* etc. − perhaps one day the heavens will have mercy on me.
13) *'Non me dir...'* etc. − don't call me beautiful, my idol.

Postscript:
Conversation at Lunch

CLEVER MAN with snuffbox, noisily closing the lid: 'How trying it is that we shall not hear a decent opera again for so long! But I put it all down to that awful exaggeration!'

MULATTO: 'Yes, indeed! I was always telling her so! The role of Donna Anna always took so much out of her. And yesterday she was more frenzied than

...since the signora died at two o'clock this morning.

ever. They say she was in a faint right through the interval, and in the scene in the second act she actually threw a fit...'

UNIMPORTANT PERSON: 'Go on, you don't say!'

MULATTO: 'Oh yes — a fit! But she wouldn't leave the theatre.'

I: 'Dear me — I hope it was nothing serious; I trust we shall soon hear the signora sing again.'

CLEVER MAN with snuffbox, taking a pinch: 'That's hardly likely, since the signora died at two o'clock this morning.'

Guy de Maupassant
HIM?

YOU can't understand it, can you, old fellow? I don't blame you. Do you think I have gone off my head? Maybe I have, a little, but not for the reasons you suppose.

Yes. I'm getting married. And that's that.

Yet I haven't changed my ideas on the subject. I still consider it stupid to get legally hitched. I'm sure eight out of ten husbands are cuckolds. Nor do they deserve any better for having been foolish enough to tie themselves

I still consider it stupid to get legally hitched.

down, to renounce love without obligation, the only thing in the world that's both gay and good, to clip the wings of that fantasy that constantly drives us towards all women, etc., etc. More than ever, I feel incapable of loving one woman, since I shall always be too much in love with all the rest. I should like to have a thousand arms, a thousand lips, a thousand... temperaments, that I might embrace a whole army of those charming and inconsequential creatures all at once.

And yet, I am getting married.

I might add that I scarcely even know my bride-to-be. I have only seen her four or five times. All I know is that she doesn't displease me in the least, and for present purposes that's enough for me. She's petite, blonde and plump. The day after tomorrow I shall ardently desire a tall, slim brunette.

She's not rich. She comes from a middle-ranking sort of family. One of those marriageable young girls, with neither anything to commend them nor any apparent faults, that are two-a-penny in the ranks of the middle classes. People say: 'That Mlle Lajolle is very pleasant.' Tomorrow they will say: 'That Mme Raymon is most pleasant.' In short, she's one of that host of respectable young ladies who 'make some man very happy' − until, that is, he realizes that he prefers all other women to the one he has chosen.

Then why get married, you ask?

I scarcely dare to divulge the strange and unlikely reason that leads me to act so unreasonably.

I am doing it so as not to be alone!

I don't know how to put it, how to make you understand. You feel sorry for me, and will disdain me, so low are my spirits.

I don't want to be alone at night any more. I want to feel another being near to me, beside me, a creature that can speak, can say something − anything.

I want to be able to wake her up; to ask her something out of the blue, something stupid, just to hear the sound of another voice. I want to feel that my home is lived-in, that there is a waking soul there, a mind at work; if I should suddenly light a candle, I want to find a human figure lying by my side... because... (how ashamed I am to admit it)... because I'm afraid on my own.

Oh! But you still don't understand.

I'm not afraid of any danger. If a man were to come in, I should kill him without turning a hair. I'm not afraid of the dead: I believe them to be gone for ever!

But... well! Well, yes! I'm afraid of myself! I'm afraid of fear, afraid of the spasms of my own frenzied soul, of a horrible sense of incomprehensible terror.

Laugh, if you like. It's awful, incurable. I'm afraid of the walls, of the furniture, of familiar objects which to me are inspired with some sort of animal life. Above all I am afraid of the terrible mess my mind is in, as my reason slips away, churned up and then flung to the winds by a mysterious and invisible anguish.

It begins with a vague disquiet which suffuses my soul and sends a chill over my skin. I look around me. Nothing! And yet I should like there to be something! What? Something comprehensible, since the only reason I am afraid is because I don't understand my fear.

I speak, and I am afraid of my own voice. I walk about, and I am afraid of something or other behind the door, behind the curtains, in the cupboard, under the bed. Yet I know there is nothing there.

I turn round suddenly, because I am afraid of what is behind me, even though there's nothing there, and I know it.

I am shaking; I feel my terror growing, and I shut myself up in my room. I get into bed and hide under the bedclothes. Crouching there, rolled up into a ball, I close my eyes in despair and remain there for an infinity, thinking that my candle is alight on the bedside table and that I must put it out. But I daren't do it.

Is it not an awful state to be in?

I never used to have such troubles. I would return home calmly. I would come and go about the flat without anything to disturb the serenity of my spirit. If anyone had told me what a morbid fear, incredible, stupid, terrifying, would one day seize me, I should have laughed at him. I used to open doors in the dark without batting an eyelid; I would take my time going to bed, and wouldn't even shoot the bolt. Nor would I get up in the middle of the night to make sure the doors and windows were securely fastened.

It all started last year, in the most peculiar way.

It was a stuffy evening in autumn. After dinner, when the maid had left, I wondered what I should do. For a while I walked about my room. I felt tired, strangely depressed, unable to work, or even to read. A fine drizzle misted the window panes; I was sad, pervaded with a sadness of the sort which comes for no reason and makes you feel like crying, makes you want to talk to anyone at all, just to relieve the weight of your own thoughts.

I felt alone. My flat seemed empty, in a way it had never done before. An infinite, heartrending solitude surrounded me. What was I to do? I sat down. Then a nervous impatience ran through my legs. I stood up again, and began to walk about. I may have had a bit of a fever, for I had my hands joined behind my back, as one does when walking slowly, and I could feel them hot against each other. Then, suddenly, a shiver of cold ran down my back. It occurred to me that the damp was getting inside the flat, and I thought I should light a fire. I did so — it was the first time that year. Then

I sat down again and watched it burning. But soon my inability to keep still had me on my feet again, and I felt I should have to go and shake myself out of it, find one of my friends.

I went out. I called on three close acquaintances, but none of them was at home. Then I made for the main street, determined to track down someone I knew.

There was a sadness everywhere. The wet pavements were shiny. The

There was a sadness everywhere. The wet pavements were shiny.

street was steeped in the sort of dampness that sends sudden shivers of cold through your body, a heavy dampness caused by an imperceptible drizzle which seemed to dim and obscure the gas-lights.

I walked along at a gentle pace, repeating to myself: 'I shan't find anyone to talk to.'

I took a look in several cafés, from the Madeleine to the Poissonnière district. The sad customers sitting at their tables seemed to lack even the strength to finish their drinks.

I wandered about like that for a long time, and towards midnight set off home. I was very calm, but very tired. The concierge, who goes to bed before eleven, opened up with unusual promptness, and I thought: 'There you are, one of the other tenants must have just returned.'

I always give two turns of the key in the lock when I leave the flat, so I was surprised to find that the door was on the latch. I presumed they had taken some mail up in the course of the evening.

I went inside. The fire I had lit was still burning, and it threw a little light around the apartment. I had picked up a candle, intending to light it at the hearth, when, glancing in front of me, I saw that there was someone sitting in my armchair with his back towards me, warming his feet in front of the fire.

I was not afraid – not in the least. A quite reasonable explanation came to mind: that one of my friends had come visiting. The wife of the concierge, whom I had informed of my departure, had told the visitor I was soon to return, and lent him her key. In an instant I recalled the circumstances of my arrival: the fact that the concierge had opened up promptly, and that my door had been on the latch.

My friend, of whom I could see only his hair, had fallen asleep while he was waiting by the fireside, and now I stepped across to wake him. I could see him perfectly, his right arm hanging down, his legs crossed, his head bowed a little against the left-hand side of the armchair, showing him to be asleep. Who is it? I wondered. It was not easy to see in that dim light. I reached out my hand to touch his shoulder...

It came to rest on the wood of the armchair! There was no one there. The chair was empty!

Great heavens – what a shock!

I recoiled as if some fearful danger had appeared before me.

Then I spun round, feeling there was someone behind me, but at once an overwhelming need to see the chair again impelled me to turn on my heels once more. And there I stood, scarcely breathing, so confused that I could not gather my thoughts. I felt ready to drop.

But I am a cold-blooded sort of fellow, and soon came to my senses. I said to myself: 'I've just had an hallucination, that's all.' And I immediately considered the phenomenon. At such moments as these one thinks quickly.

I had had an hallucination – that was an indisputable fact. Yes; my mind had remained lucid throughout, functioning properly and logically. So

Guy de Maupassant

there was nothing wrong with my brain. Only my eyes had deceived me, had deluded my mind. My eyes had had a vision, the sort that makes simple folk believe in miracles. It was just a nervous mishap to the optical apparatus, that was all — a rush of blood, maybe.

I lit my candle. As I bent down towards the fire, I noticed that I was trembling, and I righted myself with a jerk, as though someone had touched me from behind.

Who is it? I wondered. It was not easy to see in that dim light.

I was clearly not so calm after all.

I took a few steps, spoke out loud. I sang a couple of songs in a low voice.

Then I locked the door of my room with two turns of the key, and felt somewhat reassured. At least no one could get in.

I sat down again, and reflected upon my adventure for a long time. Then I got into bed and blew out the light.

For a few minutes, all was well. I lay on my back quite peacefully. Then I felt the need to look around the room, and turned on my side.

All that was left of the fire was a couple of glowing logs which sufficed to illuminate the legs of the armchair; I thought I could see the man sitting there again.

With a swift movement I lit a match. I was mistaken: I could see nothing.

Still, I got up and went to hide the armchair behind my bed.

Then I put out the light again, and tried to get off to sleep. I hadn't lost consciousness for more than five minutes when I saw, in a dream, just as it had been in reality, the whole of that evening's scene. I woke up in confusion and, after having lit up the flat again, remained sitting up in bed, not daring even to try to sleep any more.

I did, however, drop off for a few seconds a couple of times, and on each occasion I saw it all again. I thought I had gone crazy.

When day broke, I felt I was cured, and I slept soundly until noon.

That was the end of that, and no mistake. I had had a fever, or a nightmare — how should I know? In short, I had been ill. In any case, I felt a real fool.

I was in a really good mood that day. I dined at the cabaret, went to the theatre, and made my way home. But the moment I drew near my house, I was seized with a strange disquiet. I was afraid of seeing *him* again. I wasn't afraid of him as such, not afraid of his presence, which I didn't believe in, but afraid of my eyes deceiving me again, afraid of the hallucination, of the terror which would seize me.

For more than an hour I walked up and down on the pavement; then I thought myself an idiot, and finally went inside. I was so breathless I could scarcely climb the stairs. I stayed on the landing outside my flat for a good ten minutes, until, suddenly, I felt a surge of courage, a stiffening of will. I put the key in the lock and strode forward briskly with a candle in my hand, kicking open the door of my room and casting a fearful glance towards the fireplace. I saw nothing. Ah!

What a relief! What joy! What deliverance! I walked boldly up and down. But I didn't feel reassured: I kept turning suddenly, and the shadows in the corners made me feel uneasy.

I slept poorly, constantly awakened by imaginary sounds. But I didn't see him any more. No. It was over!

Since that day I have been afraid to be alone at night. I feel it there, close to me, around me — that vision. It has never come back to me. Oh, no! And what if it did, anyway, since I don't believe in it, since I know it is nothing?

Nonetheless, it bothers me, because I think about it all the time. The right hand hanging down, the head leaning to the left like that of a man asleep... Enough of that, in heaven's name! I don't want to think about it any more!

He's behind doors, in the closed cupboard, under the bed, in all the dark corners, all the shadows.

But what is this obsession? Why does it persist? His feet were right in front of the fire!

He haunts me; it's crazy, but it's true. Who, him? I know very well he doesn't exist, that he's nothing! He exists only in my apprehension, my fear, my anguish! Enough! Enough!

But it's no use reasoning with myself, telling myself I must pull myself together; I can't stay at home on my own, because he is there. I know I won't see him any more; he won't show himself — that's finished. But he's there all the same, in my mind. He remains invisible, but that doesn't make any difference to the fact that he's there. He's behind doors, in the closed cupboard, under the bed, in all the dark corners, all the shadows. If I open the door, or the cupboard, or shine a light under the bed, or light up the corners or the shadows, he isn't there any more. But I can feel him behind my back. I turn, though I know I shan't see him, that I'll never see him again. But he's still behind me, all the same.

It's stupid, but it's frightful. What am I to do? I can't help it.

But if there were two of us in the flat, I think — I'm sure — *he* wouldn't be there any more! He's there because I'm on my own, purely and simply because I'm on my own!

Edgar Allan Poe
WILLIAM WILSON

LET me call myself, for the present, William Wilson. The fair page now lying before me need not be sullied with my real appellation. This has been already too much an object for the scorn — for the horror — for the detestation of my race. To the uttermost regions of the globe, have not the indignant winds bruited its unparalleled infamy? Oh, outcast of all outcasts most abandoned! — to the earth art thou not for ever dead? to its honours to its flowers, to its golden aspirations? — and a cloud, dense, dismal, and

...art thou not for ever dead?

limitless, does it not hang eternally between thy hopes and heaven?

I would not, if I could, here or today, embody a record of my later years of unspeakable misery, and unpardonable crime. This epoch — these later years — took unto themselves a sudden elevation in turpitude, whose origin alone it is my present purpose to assign. Men usually grow base by degrees. From me, in an instant, all virtue dropped bodily as a mantle. From comparatively trivial wickedness I passed, with the stride of a giant, into more than the enormities of an Elah-Gabalus. What chance — what one event brought this evil thing to pass, bear with me while I relate. Death approaches; and the shadow which foreruns him has thrown a softening influence over my spirit. I long, in passing through the dim valley, for the sympathy — I had nearly said for the pity — of my fellow men. I would fain have them believe that I have been, in some measure, the slave of circumstances beyond human control. I would wish them to seek out for me, in the details I am about to give, some little oasis of fatality amid a wilderness of error. I would have them allow — what they cannot refrain from allowing — that, although temptation may have erewhile existed as great, man was never thus, at least, tempted before — certainly, never thus fell. And is it therefore that he has never thus suffered? Have I not indeed been living in a dream? And am I not now dying a victim to the horror and the mystery of the wildest of all sublunary visions?

I am the descendant of a race whose imaginative and easily excitable temperament has at all times rendered them remarkable; and, in my earliest infancy, I gave evidence of having fully inherited the family character. As I advanced in years it was more strongly developed; becoming for many reasons, a cause of serious disquietude to my friends, and of positive injury to myself. I grew self-willed, addicted to the wildest caprices and a prey to the most ungovernable passions. Weak-minded, and beset with constitutional infirmities akin to my own, my parents could do but little to check the evil propensities which distinguished me. Some feeble and ill-directed efforts resulted in complete failure on their part, and, of course, in total triumph on mine. Thenceforward my voice was a household law; and at an age when few children have abandoned their leading-strings, I was left to the guidance of my own will, and became, in all but name, the master of my own actions.

My earliest recollections of a school-life, are connected with a large, rambling, Elizabethan house, in a misty-looking village of England, where were a vast number of gigantic and gnarled trees, and where all the houses were excessively ancient. In truth, it was a dream-like and spirit-soothing place, that venerable old town. At this moment, in fancy, I feel the refreshing chilliness of its deeply-shadowed avenues, inhale the fragrance of its thousand shrubberies, and thrill anew with undefinable delight, at the deep hollow note of the church-bell, breaking, each hour, with sullen and sudden roar, upon the stillness of the dusky atmosphere in which the fretted Gothic steeple lay imbedded and asleep.

It gives me, perhaps, as much of pleasure as I can now in any manner experience, to dwell upon minute recollections of the school and its concerns. Steeped in misery as I am — misery, alas! only too real — I shall be pardoned for seeking relief, however slight and temporary, in the weakness of a few rambling details. These, moreover, utterly trivial, and even ridiculous in themselves, assume, to my fancy, adventitious importance, as connected with a period and locality when and where I recognize the first ambiguous monitions of the destiny which afterward so fully overshadowed me. Let me then remember.

The house, I have said, was old and irregular. The grounds were extensive, and a high and solid brick wall, topped with a bed of mortar and broken glass, encompassed the whole. This prison-like rampart formed the limit of our domain; beyond it we saw but thrice a week — once every Saturday afternoon, when, attended by two ushers, we were permitted to take brief walks in a body through some of the neighbouring fields — and twice during Sunday, when we were paraded in the same formal manner to the morning and evening service in the one church of the village. Of this church the principal of our school was pastor. With how deep a spirit of wonder and perplexity was I wont to regard him from our remote pew in the gallery, as, with step solemn and slow, he ascended the pulpit! This reverend man with countenance so demurely benign, with robes so glossy and so clerically flowing, with wig so minutely powdered, so rigid and so vast, — could this be he who, of late, with sour visage, and in snuffy habiliments, administered, ferule in hand, the Draconian Laws of the academy? Oh, gigantic paradox, too utterly monstrous for solution!

At an angle of the ponderous wall frowned a more ponderous gate. It was riveted and studded with iron bolts, and surmounted with jagged iron spikes. What impressions of deep awe did it inspire! It was never opened save for the three periodical egressions and ingressions already mentioned; then, in every creak of its mighty hinges, we found a plenitude of mystery — a world of matter for solemn remark, or for more solemn meditation.

The extensive enclosure was irregular in form, having many capacious recesses. Of these, three or four of the largest constituted the play-ground. It was level, and covered with fine hard gravel. I well remember it had no trees, nor benches, nor any thing similar within it. Of course it was in the rear of the house. In front lay a small parterre, planted with box and other shrubs, but through this sacred division we passed only upon rare occasions indeed — such as a first advent to school or final departure thence, or perhaps, when a parent or friend having called for us, we joyfully took our way home for the Christmas or Midsummer holidays.

But the house! — how quaint an old building was this! — to me how veritably a palace of enchantment! There was really no end to its windings — to its incomprehensible subdivisions. It was difficult, at any given time, to say with certainty upon which of its two stories one happened to be. From each room to every other there were sure to be found three or four steps either in ascent or descent. Then the lateral branches were innumerable — inconceivable — and so returning in upon themselves, that our most exact ideas in regard to the whole mansion were not very far different from those with which we pondered upon infinity. During the five years of my residence here, I was never able to ascertain with precision, in what remote locality lay the little sleeping apartment assigned to myself and some eighteen or twenty other scholars.

The school-room was the largest in the house — I could not help thinking, in the world. It was very long, narrow, and dismally low, with pointed Gothic windows and a ceiling of oak. In a remote and terror-inspiring angle was a square enclosure of eight or ten feet, comprising the sanctum, 'during hours,' of our principal, the Reverend Dr Bransby. It was a solid structure, with massy door, sooner than open which in the absence of the 'Dominie,' we would all have willingly perished by the _peine forte et dure_. In other angles were two other similar boxes, far less reverenced, indeed, but still greatly matters of awe. One of these was the pulpit of the 'classical' usher, one of the 'English and mathematical.' Interspersed about the room, crossing and recrossing in endless irregularity, were innumerable benches and desks, black, ancient, and time-worn, piled desperately with much bethumbed books, and so beseamed with initial letters, names at full length, grotesque figures, and other multiplied efforts of the knife, as to have entirely lost what little of original form might have been their portion in days long departed. A huge bucket with water stood at one extremity of the room, and a clock of stupendous dimensions at the other.

Encompassed by the massy walls of this venerable academy, I passed yet not in tedium or disgust, the years of the third lustrum of my life. The teeming brain of childhood requires no external world of incident to occupy or amuse it; and the apparently dismal monotony of a school was replete with more intense excitement than my riper youth has derived from luxury, or my full manhood from crime. Yet I must believe that my first mental development had in it much of the uncommon — even much of the outré.

Upon mankind at large the events of very early existence rarely leave in mature age any definite impression. All is grey shadow — weak and irregular remembrance — an indistinct regathering of feeble pleasures and phantasmagoric pains. With me this is not so. In childhood I must have felt with the energy of a man what I now find stamped upon memory in lines as vivid, as deep, and as durable as the exergues of the Carthaginian medals.

Yet in fact — in the fact of the world's view — how little was there to

...piled desperately with much bethumbed books...

remember! The morning's awakening, the nightly summons to bed; the connings, the recitations; the periodical half-holidays, and perambulations; the playground, with its broils, its pastimes, its intrigues; — these, by a mental sorcery long forgotten, were made to involve a wilderness of sensation, a world of rich incident, an universe of varied emotion, of excitement the most passionate and spirit-stirring. *'Oh, le bon temps, que ce siècle de fer!'*

In truth, the ardour, the enthusiasm, and the imperiousness of my disposition, soon rendered me a marked character among my schoolmates, and by slow, but natural gradations, gave me an ascendancy over all not greatly older than myself; — over all with a single exception. This exception was found in the person of a scholar, who, although no relation, bore the same Christian and surname as myself; — a circumstance, in fact, little remarkable; for, notwithstanding a noble descent, mine was one of those everyday appellations which seem, by prescriptive right, to have been, time out of mind, the common property of the mob. In this narrative I have therefore designated myself as William Wilson, — a fictitious title not very dissimilar to the real. My namesake alone, of those who in school phraseology constituted 'our set', presumed to compete with me in the studies of the class — in the sports and broils of the playground — to refuse implicit belief in my assertions, and submission to my will — indeed, to interfere with my arbitrary dictation in any respect whatsoever. If there is on earth a supreme and unqualified despotism, it is the despotism of a mastermind in boyhood over the less energetic spirits of its companions.

Wilson's rebellion was to me a source of the greatest embarrassment; the more so as, in spite of the bravado with which in public I made a point of treating him and his pretensions, I secretly felt that I feared him, and could not help thinking the equality which he maintained so easily with myself, a proof of his true superiority; since not to be overcome, cost me a perpetual struggle. Yet this superiority — even this equality — was in truth acknowledged by no one but myself; our associates, by some unaccountable blindness, seemed not even to suspect it. Indeed, his competition, his resistance, and especially his impertinent and dogged interference with my purposes, were not more pointed than private. He appeared to be destitute alike of the ambition which urged, and of the passionate energy of mind which enabled me to excel. In his rivalry he might have been supposed actuated solely by a whimsical desire to thwart, astonish, or mortify myself; although there were times when I could not help observing, with a feeling made up of wonder, abasement, and pique, that he mingled with his injuries, his insults, or his contradictions, a certain most inappropriate, and assuredly most unwelcome affectionateness of manner. I could only conceive this singular behaviour to arise from a consummate self-conceit assuming the vulgar airs of patronage and protection.

Perhaps it was this latter trait in Wilson's conduct, conjoined with our identity of name, and the mere accident of our having entered the school upon the same day, which set afloat the notion that we were brothers, among the senior classes in the academy. These do not usually inquire with much strictness into the affairs of their juniors. I have before said, or should have said, that Wilson was not, in a most remote degree, connected with my family. But assuredly if we had been brothers we must have been twins; for, after leaving Dr Bransby's, I casually learned that my namesake was born on the nineteenth of January, 1813 − and this is a somewhat remarkable coincidence; for the day is precisely that of my own nativity.

It may seem strange that in spite of the continual anxiety occasioned me by the rivalry of Wilson, and his intolerable spirit of contradiction, I could not bring myself to hate him altogether. We had, to be sure, nearly every day a quarrel in which, yielding me publicly the palm of victory, he, in some manner, contrived to make me feel that it was he who had deserved it; yet a sense of pride on my part, and a veritable dignity on his own, kept us always upon what are called 'speaking terms', while there were many points of strong congeniality in our tempers, operating to awake in me a sentiment which our position alone, perhaps, prevented from ripening into friendship. It is difficult, indeed, to define, or even to describe, my real feelings toward him. They formed a motley and heterogeneous admixture; − some petulant animosity, which was not yet hatred, some esteem, more respect, much fear, with a world of uneasy curiosity. To the moralist it will be necessary to say, in addition, that Wilson and myself were the most inseparable of companions.

It was no doubt the anomalous state of affairs existing between us, which turned all my attacks upon him (and there were many, either open or covert) into the channel of banter or practical joke (giving pain while assuming the aspect of mere fun) rather than into a more serious and determined hostility. But my endeavours on this head were by no means uniformly successful, even when my plans were the most wittily concocted; for my namesake had much about him, in character, of that unassuming and quiet austerity which, while enjoying the poignancy of its own jokes, has no heel of Achilles in itself, and absolutely refuses to be laughed at. I could find, indeed, but one vulnerable point, and that, lying in a personal peculiarity, arising, perhaps, from constitutional disease, would have been spared by any antagonist less at his wits' end than myself; my rival had a weakness in the faucial or guttural organs, which precluded him from raising his voice at any time above a very low whisper. Of this defect I did not fail to take what poor advantage lay in my power.

Wilson's retaliations in kind were many; and there was one form of his practical wit that disturbed me beyond measure. How his sagacity first discovered at all that so petty a thing would vex me, is a question I never could solve; but having discovered, he habitually practised the annoyance. I had always felt aversion to my uncourtly patronymic, and its very common, if not plebeian praenomen. The words were venom in my ears; and when, upon the day of my arrival, a second William Wilson came also to the academy, I felt angry with him for bearing the name, and doubly disgusted with the name because a stranger bore it, who would be the cause of its twofold repetition, who would be constantly in my presence, and whose concerns, in the ordinary routine of the school business, must inevitably, on account of the detestable coincidence, be often confounded with my own.

The feeling of vexation thus engendered grew stronger with every circumstance tending to show resemblance, moral or physical, between my rival and myself. I had not then discovered the remarkable fact that we were of the same age; but I saw that we were of the same height, and I perceived that we were even singularly alike in general contour of person and outline of feature. I was galled, too, by the rumour touching a relationship, which had grown current in the upper forms. In a word, nothing could more seriously disturb me (although I scrupulously concealed such disturbance) than any allusion to a similarity of mind, person, or condition existing between us. But, in truth, I had no reason to believe that (with the exception of the matter of relationship, and in the case of Wilson himself) this similarity had ever been made a subject of comment, or even observed at all by our schoolfellows. That he observed it in all its bearings, and as fixedly as I, was apparent; but that he could discover in such circumstances so fruitful a field of annoyance, can only be attributed, as I said before, to his more than ordinary penetration.

His cue, which was to perfect an imitation of myself, lay both in words and in actions; and most admirably did he play his part. My dress it was an easy matter to copy; my gait and general manner were without difficulty, appropriated; in spite of his constitutional defect, even my voice did not escape him. My louder tones were, of course, unattempted, but then the key, — it was identical; and his singular whisper, it grew the very echo of my own.

How greatly this most exquisite portraiture harassed me (for it could not justly be termed a caricature), I will not now venture to describe. I had but one consolation — in the fact that the imitation, apparently, was noticed by myself alone, and that I had to endure only the knowing and strangely sarcastic smiles of my namesake himself. Satisfied with having produced in my bosom the intended effect, he seemed to chuckle in secret over the sting he had inflicted, and was characteristically disregardful of the public applause which the success of his witty endeavours might have so easily elicited. That the school, indeed, did not feel his design, perceive its accomplishment, and participate in his sneer, was, for many anxious months, a riddle I could not resolve. Perhaps the gradation of his copy rendered it not readily perceptible; or, more possibly, I owed my security to the masterly air of the copyist, who, disdaining the letter (which in a painting is all the obtuse can see), gave but the full spirit of his original for my individual contemplation and chagrin.

I have already more than once spoken of the disgusting air of patronage which he assumed toward me, and of his frequent officious interference with my will. This interference often took the ungracious character of advice; advice not openly given, but hinted or insinuated. I received it with a repugnance which gained strength as I grew in years. Yet, at this distant day, let me do him the simple justice to acknowledge that I can recall no occasion when the suggestions of my rival were on the side of those errors or follies so usual to his immature age and seeming inexperience; that his moral sense, at least, if not his general talents and worldly wisdom, was far keener than my own; and that I might, today, have been a better and thus a happier man, had I less frequently rejected the counsels embodied in those meaning whispers which I then but too cordially hated and too bitterly despised.

As it was I at length grew restive in the extreme under his distasteful supervision, and daily resented more and more openly, what I considered his intolerable arrogance. I have said that, in the first years of our connection as schoolmates, my feelings in regard to him might have been easily ripened into friendship; but, in the latter months of my residence at the academy, although the intrusion of his ordinary manner had, beyond doubt, in some measure, abated, my sentiments, in nearly similar proportion, partook very much of positive hatred. Upon one occasion he saw this, I think, and afterward avoided, or made a show of avoiding me.

It was about the same period, if I remember aright, that, in an altercation of violence with him, in which he was more than usually thrown off his guard, and spoke and acted with an openness of demeanour rather

Edgar Allan Poe

foreign to his nature, I discovered, or fancied I discovered, in his accent, in his air, and general appearance, a something which first startled, and then deeply interested me, by bringing to mind dim visions of my earliest infancy – wild, confused, and thronging memories of a time when memory herself was yet unborn. I cannot better describe the sensation which oppressed me, than by saying that I could with difficulty shake off the belief of my having been acquainted with the being who stood before me, at some epoch very long ago – some point of the past even infinitely remote. The delusion, however, faded rapidly as it came; and I mention it at all but to define the day of the last conversation I there held with my singular namesake.

The huge old house, with its countless subdivisions, had several large chambers communicating with each other, where slept the greater number of the students. There were, however (as must necessarily happen in a building so awkwardly planned), many little nooks or recesses, the odds and ends of the structure; and these the economic ingenuity of Dr Bransby had also fitted up as dormitories; although, being the merest closets, they were capable of accommodating but a single individual. One of these small apartments was occupied by Wilson.

One night, about the close of my fifth year at the school, and immediately after the altercation just mentioned, finding every one wrapped in sleep, I arose from bed, and, lamp in hand, stole through a wilderness of narrow passages, from my own bedroom to that of my rival. I had long been plotting one of those ill-natured pieces of practical wit at his expense in which I had hitherto been so uniformly unsuccessful. It was my intention, now, to put my scheme in operation and I resolved to make him feel the whole extent of the malice with which I was imbued. Having reached his closet, I noiselessly entered, leaving the lamp, with a shade over it, on the outside. I advanced a step and listened to the sound of his tranquil breathing. Assured of his being asleep, I returned, took the light, and with it again approached the bed. Close curtains were around it, which, in the prosecution of my plan, I slowly and quietly withdrew, when the bright rays fell vividly upon the sleeper, and my eyes at the same moment, upon his countenance. I looked; – and a numbness, an iciness of feeling instantly pervaded my frame. My breast heaved, my knees tottered, my whole spirit became possessed with an objectless yet intolerable horror. Gasping for breath, I lowered the lamp in still nearer proximity to the face. Were these – these the lineaments of William Wilson? I saw, indeed, that they were his, but I shook as if with a fit of the ague, in fancying they were not. What was there about them to confound me in this manner? I gazed; — while my brain reeled with a multitude of incoherent thoughts. Not thus he appeared — assuredly not thus — in the vivacity of his waking hours. The same name! the same contour of person! the same day of arrival at the academy! And then his dogged and meaningless imitation of my gait, my voice, my habits, and my manner! Was it, in truth, within the bounds of human possibility, that what I now saw was the result, merely, of the habitual practice of this

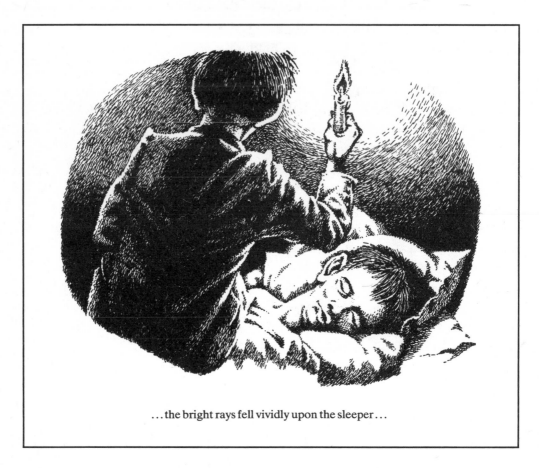

...the bright rays fell vividly upon the sleeper...

sarcastic imitation? Awe-stricken, and with a creeping shudder, I extinguished the lamp, passed silently from the chamber, and left, at once, the halls of that old academy, never to enter them again.

After a lapse of some months, spent at home in mere idleness, I found myself a student at Eton. The brief interval had been sufficient to enfeeble my remembrance of the events at Dr Bransby's, or at least to effect a material change in the nature of the feelings with which I remembered them. The truth — the tragedy — of the drama was no more. I could now find room to doubt the evidence of my senses; and seldom called up the subject at all but with wonder at the extent of human credulity, and a smile at the vivid force of the imagination which I hereditarily possessed. Neither was this species of scepticism likely to be diminished by the character of the life I led at Eton. The vortex of thoughtless folly into which I there so immediately and so recklessly plunged, washed away all but the froth of my past hours, ingulfed at once every solid or serious impression, and left to memory only the veriest levities of a former existence.

I do not wish, however, to trace the course of my miserable profligacy here — a profligacy which set at defiance the laws, while it eluded the vigilance of the institution. Three years of folly, passed without profit, had but given me rooted habits of vice, and added, in a somewhat unusual degree, to my bodily stature, when, after a week of soulless dissipation, I invited a small party of the most dissolute students to a secret carousal in my chambers. We met at a late hour of the night; for our debaucheries were to be faithfully protracted until morning. The wine flowed freely, and there were not wanting other and perhaps more dangerous seductions; so that the gray dawn had already faintly appeared in the east while our delirious extravagance was at its height. Madly flushed with cards and intoxication, I was in the act of insisting upon a toast of more than wonted profanity, when my attention was suddenly diverted by the violent, although partial, unclosing of the door of the apartment, and by the eager voice of a servant from without. He said that some person, apparently in great haste, demanded to speak with me in the hall.

Wildly excited with wine, the unexpected interruption rather delighted than surprised me. I staggered forward at once, and a few steps brought me to the vestibule of the building. In this low and small room there hung no lamp; and now no light at all was admitted, save that of the exceedingly feeble dawn which made its way through the semi-circular window. As I put my foot over the threshold, I became aware of the figure of a youth about my own height, and habited in a white kerseymere morning frock, cut in the novel fashion of the one I myself wore at the moment. This the faint light enabled me to perceive; but the features of his face I could not distinguish. Upon my entering, he strode hurriedly up to me, and, seizing me by the arm with a gesture of petulant impatience, whispered the words 'William Wilson' in my ear.

I grew perfectly sober in an instant.

There was that in the manner of the stranger, and in the tremulous shake of his uplifted finger, as he held it between my eyes and the light, which filled me with unqualified amazement; but it was not this which had so violently moved me. It was the pregnancy of solemn admonition in the singular, low, hissing utterance; and, above all, it was the character, the tone, the key, of those few, simple, and familiar, yet whispered syllables, which came with a thousand thronging memories of bygone days, and struck upon my soul with the shock of a galvanic battery. Ere I could recover the use of my senses he was gone.

Although this event failed not of a vivid effect upon my disordered imagination, yet was it evanescent as vivid. For some weeks, indeed, I busied myself in earnest inquiry, or was wrapped in a cloud of morbid speculation. I did not pretend to disguise from my perception the identity of the singular individual who thus perseveringly interfered with my affairs, and harassed me with his insinuated counsel. But who and what was this Wilson? − and whence came he? − and what were his purposes? Upon neither of these points could I be satisfied − merely ascertaining, in regard to him, that a sudden accident in his family had caused his removal from Dr Bransby's academy on the afternoon of the day in which I myself had eloped. But in a brief period I ceased to think upon the subject, my attention being all absorbed in a contemplated departure for Oxford. Thither I soon went, the uncalculating vanity of my parents furnishing me with an outfit and annual establishment, which would enable me to indulge at will in the luxury already so dear to my heart − to vie in profuseness of expenditure with the haughtiest heirs of the wealthiest earldoms in Great Britain.

Excited by such appliances to vice, my constitutional temperament broke forth with redoubled ardour, and I spurned even the common restraints of decency in the mad infatuation of my revels. But it were absurd to pause in the detail of my extravagance. Let it suffice, that among spendthrifts I out-Heroded Herod, and that, giving name to a multitude of novel follies, I added no brief appendix to the long catalogue of vices then usual in the most dissolute university of Europe.

It could hardly be credited, however, that I had, even here, so utterly fallen from the gentlemanly estate, as to seek acquaintance with the vilest arts of the gambler by profession, and, having become an adept in his despicable science, to practice it habitually as a means of increasing my already enormous income at the expense of the weak-minded among my fellow-collegians. Such, nevertheless, was the fact. And the very enormity of this offence against all manly and honourable sentiment proved, beyond doubt, the main if not the sole reason of the impunity with which it was committed. Who, indeed, among my most abandoned associates, would not rather have disputed the clearest evidence of his senses, than have suspected of such courses, the gay, the frank, the generous William Wilson — the noblest and most liberal commoner at Oxford — him whose follies

...as to seek acquaintance with the vilest arts of the gambler by profession...

(said his parasites) were but the follies of youth and unbridled fancy — whose errors but inimitable whim — whose darkest vice but a careless and dashing extravagance?

I had been now two years successfully busied in this way, when there came to the university a young parvenu nobleman, Glendinning — rich, said report, as Herodes Atticus — his riches, too, as easily acquired. I soon found him of weak intellect, and, of course, marked him as a fitting subject for my skill. I frequently engaged him in play, and contrived, with the gambler's usual art, to let him win considerable sums, the more effectually to entangle him in my snares. At length, my schemes being ripe, I met him (with the full intention that this meeting should be final and decisive) at the chambers of a fellow-commoner (Mr Preston), equally intimate with both, but who, to do him justice, entertained not even a remote suspicion of my design. To give to this a better colouring, I had contrived to have assembled a party of some eight or ten, and was solicitously careful that the introduction of cards should appear accidental, and originate in the proposal of my contemplated dupe himself. To be brief upon a vile topic, none of the low finesse was omitted, so customary upon similar occasions, that it is a just matter for wonder how any are still found so besotted as to fall its victim.

We had protracted our sitting far into the night, and I had at length effected the manoeuvre of getting Glendinning as my sole antagonist. The game, too, was my favourite *écarté*. The rest of the company, interested in the extent of our play, had abandoned their own cards, and were standing around us as spectators. The *parvenu*, who had been induced by my artifices in the early part of the evening, to drink deeply, now shuffled, dealt, or played, with a wild nervousness of manner of which his intoxication, I thought, might partially, but could not altogether account. In a very short period he had become my debtor to a large amount, when, having taken a long draught of port, he did precisely what I had been coolly anticipating – he proposed to double our already extravagant stakes. With a well-feigned show of reluctance, and not until after my repeated refusal had seduced him into some angry words which gave a colour of pique to my compliance, did I finally comply. The result, of course, did but prove how entirely the prey was in my toils: in less than an hour he had quadrupled his debt. For some time his countenance had been losing the florid tinge lent it by the wine; but now, to my astonishment, I perceived that it had grown to a pallor truly fearful. I say to my astonishment. Glendinning had been represented to my eager inquiries as immeasurably wealthy; and the sums which he had as yet lost, although in themselves vast, could not, I supposed, very seriously annoy, much less so violently affect him. That he was overcome by the wine just swallowed, was the idea which most readily presented itself; and, rather with a view to the preservation of my own character in the eyes of my associates, than from any less interested motive, I was about to insist, peremptorily, upon a discontinuance of the play, when some expressions at my elbow from among the company, and an ejaculation evincing utter despair on the part of Glendinning, gave me to understand that I had effected his total ruin under circumstances which, rendering him an object for the pity of all, should have protected him from the ill offices even of a fiend.

What now might have been my conduct it is difficult to say. The pitiable condition of my dupe had thrown an air of embarrassed gloom over all; and, for some moments, a profound silence was maintained, during which I could not help feeling my cheeks tingle with the many burning glances of scorn or reproach cast upon me by the less abandoned of the party. I will even own that an intolerable weight of anxiety was for a brief instant lifted from my bosom by the sudden and extraordinary interruption which ensued. The wide, heavy folding doors of the apartment were all at once thrown open, to their full extent, with a vigorous and rushing impetuosity that extinguished, as if by magic, every candle in the room. Their light, in dying, enabled us just to perceive that a stranger had entered, about my own height, and closely muffled in a cloak. The darkness, however, was not total; and we could only feel that he was standing in our midst. Before any one of us could recover from the extreme astonishment into which this rudeness had thrown all, we heard the voice of the intruder.

'Gentlemen,' he said, in a low, distinct, and never-to-be-forgotten whisper which thrilled to the very marrow of my bones, 'Gentlemen, I make an apology for this behaviour, because in thus behaving, I am fulfilling a duty. You are, beyond doubt, uninformed of the true character of the person who has tonight won at *écarté* a large sum of money from Lord Glendinning. I will therefore put you upon an expeditious and decisive plan of obtaining this very necessary information. Please to examine, at your leisure, the inner linings of the cuff of his left sleeve, and the several little packages which may be found in the somewhat capacious pockets of his embroidered morning wrapper.'

While he spoke, so profound was the stillness that one might have heard a pin drop upon the floor. In ceasing, he departed at once, and as abruptly as he had entered. Can I — shall I describe my sensations? Must I say that I felt all the horrors of the damned? Most assuredly I had little time for reflection. Many hands roughly seized me upon the spot, and lights were immediately reprocured. A search ensued. In the lining of my sleeve were found all the court cards essential in *écarté*, and, in the pockets of my wrapper, a number of packs, facsimiles of those used at our sittings, with the single exception that mine were of the species called, technically, *arrondees;* the honours being slightly convex at the ends, the lower cards slightly convex at the sides. In this disposition, the dupe who cuts, as customary, at the length of the pack, will invariably find that he cuts his antagonist an honour; while the gambler, cutting at the breadth, will, as certainly, cut nothing for his victim which may count in the records of the game.

Any burst of indignation upon this discovery would have affected me less than the silent contempt, or the sarcastic composure, with which it was received.

'Mr Wilson,' said our host, stooping to remove from beneath his feet an exceedingly luxurious cloak of rare furs, 'Mr Wilson, this is your property.' (The weather was cold; and, upon quitting my own room, I had thrown a cloak over my dressing wrapper, putting it off upon reaching the scene of play.) 'I presume it is supererogatory to seek here (eyeing the folds of the garment with a bitter smile) for any farther evidence of your skill. Indeed, we have had enough. You will see the necessity, I hope, of quitting Oxford − at all events, of quitting instantly my chambers.'

Abased, humbled to the dust as I then was, it is probable that I should have resented this galling language by immediate personal violence, had not my whole attention been at the moment arrested by a fact of the most startling character. The cloak which I had worn was of a rare description of fur; how rare, how extravagantly costly, I shall not venture to say. Its fashion; too, was of my own fantastic invention; for I was fastidious to an absurd degree of coxcombry, in matters of this frivolous nature. When, therefore, Mr Preston reached me that which he had picked up upon the floor, and near the folding-doors of the apartment, it was with an astonishment nearly bordering upon terror, that I perceived my own already hanging on my arm (where I had no doubt unwittingly placed it), and that the one presented to me was but its exact counterpart in every, in even the minutest possible particular. The singular being who had so disastrously exposed me, had been muffled, I remembered, in a cloak; and none had been worn at all by any of the members of our party, with the exception of myself. Retaining some presence of mind, I took the one offered to me by Preston; placed it, unnoticed over my own; left the apartment with a resolute scowl of defiance; and, next morning ere dawn of day, commenced a hurried journey from Oxford to the Continent, in a perfect agony of horror and of shame.

I fled in vain. My evil destiny pursued me as if in exultation, and proved, indeed, that the exercise of its mysterious dominion had as yet only

Edgar Allan Poe

begun. Scarcely had I set foot in Paris, ere I had fresh evidence of the detestable interest taken by this Wilson in my concerns. Years flew, while I experienced no relief. Villain! − at Rome, with how untimely, yet with how spectral an officiousness, stepped he in between me and my ambition! at Vienna, too − at Berlin − and at Moscow! Where, in truth, had I not bitter cause to curse him within my heart? From his inscrutable tyranny did I at length flee, panic-stricken, as from a pestilence; and to the very ends of the earth I fled in vain.

And again, and again, in secret communion with my own spirit, would I demand the questions 'Who is he? − whence came he? − and what are his objects?' But no answer was there found. And now I scrutinized, with a minute scrutiny, the forms, and the methods, and the leading traits of his impertinent supervision. But even here there was very little upon which to base a conjecture. It was noticeable, indeed, that, in no one of the multiplied instances in which he had of late crossed my path, had he so crossed it except to frustrate those schemes, or to disturb those actions; which, if fully carried out, might have resulted in bitter mischief. Poor justification this, in truth, for an authority so imperiously assumed! Poor indemnity for natural rights of self-agency so pertinaciously, so insultingly denied!

I had also been forced to notice that my tormentor, for a very long period of time (while scrupulously and with miraculous dexterity maintaining his whim of an identity of apparel with myself) had so contrived it, in the execution of his varied interference with my will, that I saw not, at any moment, the features of his face. Be Wilson what he might, this, at least, was but the veriest of affectation, or of folly. Could he, for an instant, have supposed that, in my admonisher at Eton − in the destroyer of my honour at Oxford, − in him who thwarted my ambition at Rome, my revenge at Paris, my passionate love at Naples, or what he falsely termed my avarice in Egypt, − that in this, my arch-enemy and evil genius, I could fail to recognize the William Wilson of my school-boy days, − the namesake, the companion, the rival, − the hated and dreaded rival at Dr Bransby's? Impossible! − But let me hasten to the last eventful scene of the drama.

Thus far I had succumbed supinely to this imperious domination. The sentiment of deep awe with which I habitually regarded the elevated character, the majestic wisdom, the apparent omnipresence and omnipotence of Wilson, added to a feeling of even terror, with which certain other traits in his nature and assumptions inspired me, had operated, hitherto, to impress me with an idea of my own utter weakness and helplessness, and to suggest an implicit, although bitterly reluctant submission to his arbitrary will. But, of late days, I had given myself up entirely to wine; and its maddening influence upon my hereditary temper rendered me more and more impatient of control. I began to murmur, − to hesitate, − to resist. And was it only fancy which induced me to believe that, with the increase of my own firmness, that of my tormentor underwent a proportional

...that I saw not, at any moment, the features of his face.

diminution? Be this as it may, I now began to feel the inspiration of a burning hope, and at length nurtured in my secret thoughts a stern and desperate resolution that I would submit no longer to be enslaved.

It was at Rome, during the Carnival of 18−, that I attended a masquerade in the palazzo of the Neapolitan Duke Di Broglio. I had indulged more freely than usual in the excesses of the wine-table; and now the suffocating atmosphere of the crowded rooms irritated me beyond endurance. The difficulty, too, of forcing my way through the mazes of the company contributed not a little to the ruffling of my temper; for I was anxiously seeking (let me not say with what unworthy motive) the young, the gay, the beautiful wife of the aged and doting Di Broglio. With a too unscrupulous confidence she had previously communicated to me the secret of the costume in which she would be habited, and now, having caught a glimpse of her person, I was hurrying to make my way into her presence. At this moment I felt a light hand placed upon my shoulder, and that ever-remembered, low, damnable whisper within my ear.

In an absolute frenzy of wrath, I turned at once upon him who had thus interrupted me, and seized him violently by the collar. He was attired, as I had expected, in a costume altogether similar to my own; wearing a Spanish cloak of blue velvet, begirt about the waist with a crimson belt sustaining a rapier. A mask of black silk entirely covered his face.

'Scoundrel!' I said, in a voice husky with rage, while every syllable I uttered seemed as new fuel to my fury; 'Scoundrel! impostor! accursed villain! you shall not — you shall not dog me unto death! Follow me, or I stab you where you stand!' — and I broke my way from the ballroom into a small antechamber adjoining, dragging him unresistingly with me as I went.

Upon entering, I thrust him furiously from me. He staggered against the wall, while I closed the door with an oath, and commanded him to draw. He hesitated but for an instant; then, with a slight sigh, drew in silence, and put himself upon his defence.

The contest was brief indeed. I was frantic with every species of wild excitement, and felt within my single arm the energy and power of a multitude. In a few seconds I forced him by sheer strength against the wainscotting, and thus, getting him at mercy, plunged my sword, with brute ferocity, repeatedly through and through his bosom.

At that instant some person tried the latch of the door. I hastened to prevent an intrusion, and then immediately returned to my dying antagonist. But what human language can adequately portray that astonishment, that horror which possessed me at the spectacle then presented to view? The brief moment in which I averted my eyes had been sufficient to produce, apparently, a material change in the arrangements at the upper or farther end of the room. A large mirror, — so at first it seemed to me in my confusion — now stood where none had been perceptible before; and as I stepped up to it in extremity of terror, mine own image, but with features all pale and dabbled in blood, advanced to meet me with a feeble and tottering gait.

Thus it appeared, I say, but was not. It was my antagonist — it was Wilson, who then stood before me in the agonies of his dissolution. His mask and cloak lay, where he had thrown them, upon the floor. Not a thread in all his raiment — not a line in all the marked and singular lineaments of his face which was not, even in the most absolute identity, mine own!

It was Wilson; but he spoke no longer in a whisper, and I could have fancied that I myself was speaking while he said:

'You have conquered, and I yield. Yet henceforward art thou also dead — dead to the World, to Heaven, and to Hope! In me didst thou exist — and, in my death, see by this image, which is thine own, how utterly thou hast murdered thyself.'

...see by this image, which is thine own, how utterly thou hast murdered thyself.'

Anton Pavlovich Chekhov
THE BLACK MONK

ANDREY Vasselitch Kovrin, who held a master's degree at the University, had exhausted himself, and had upset his nerves. He did not send for a doctor, but casually, over a bottle of wine, he spoke to a friend who was a doctor, and the latter advised him to spend the spring and summer in the country. Very opportunely a long letter came from Tanya Pesotsky, who asked him to come and stay with them at Borissovka. And he made up his mind that he really must go.

To begin with — that was in April — he went to his own home, Kovrinka, and there spent three weeks in solitude; then, as soon as the roads were in good condition, he set off, driving in a carriage, to visit Pesotsky, his former guardian, who had brought him up, and was a horticulturalist well known all over Russia. The distance from Kovrinka to Borissovka was reckoned only a little over fifty miles. To drive along a soft road in May in a comfortable carriage with springs was a real pleasure.

Pesotsky had an immense house with columns and lions, off which the stucco was peeling, and with a footman in swallow-tails at the entrance. The old park, laid out in the English style, gloomy and severe, stretched for almost three-quarters of a mile to the river, and there ended in a steep, precipitous clay bank, where pines grew with bare roots that looked like shaggy paws; the water shone below with an unfriendly gleam, and the peewits flew up with a plaintive cry, and there one always felt that one must sit down and write a ballad. But near the house itself, in the courtyard and orchard, which together with the nurseries covered ninety acres, it was all life and gaiety even in bad weather. Such marvellous roses, lilies, camellias; such tulips of all possible shades, from glistening white to sooty black — such a wealth of flowers, in fact, Kovrin had never seen anywhere as at Pesotsky's. It was only the beginning of spring, and the real glory of the flower-beds was still hidden away in the hothouses. But even the flowers along the avenues, and here and there in the flower-beds, were enough to make one feel, as one walked about the garden, as though one were in a realm of tender colours, especially in the early morning when the dew was glistening on every petal.

What was the decorative part of the garden, and what Pesotsky contemptuously spoke of as rubbish, had at one time in his childhood given Kovrin an impression of fairyland.

Every sort of caprice, of elaborate monstrosity and mockery at Nature was here. There were espaliers of fruit-trees, a pear-tree in the shape of a pyramidal poplar, spherical oaks and lime-trees, an apple-tree in the shape of an umbrella, plum-trees trained into arches, crests, candelabra, and even into the number 1862 — the year when Pesotsky first took up horticulture. One came across, too, lovely, graceful trees with strong, straight stems like palms, and it was only by looking intently that one could recognize these trees as gooseberries or currants. But what made the garden most cheerful and gave it a lively air, was the continual coming and going in it, from early morning till evening; people with wheelbarrows, shovels, and

Such marvellous roses, lilies, camellias...

watering-cans swarmed round the trees and bushes, in the avenues and the flower-beds, like ants...

Kovrin arrived at Pesotsky's at ten o'clock in the evening. He found Tanya and her father, Yegor Semyonitch, in great anxiety. The clear starlight sky and the thermometer foretold a frost towards morning, and meanwhile Ivan Karlitch, the gardener, had gone to the town, and they had no one to rely upon. At supper they talked of nothing but the morning frost, and it was settled that Tanya should not go to bed, and between twelve and one should walk through the garden, and see that everything was done properly, and Yegor Semyonitch should get up at three o'clock or even earlier.

Kovrin sat with Tanya all the evening, and after midnight went out with her into the garden. It was cold. There was a strong smell of burning already in the garden. In the big orchard, which was called the commercial garden, and which brought Yegor Semyónitch several thousand clear profit, a thick, black, acrid smoke was creeping over the ground and, curling round the trees, was saving those thousands from the frost. Here the trees were arranged as on a chessboard, in straight and regular rows like ranks of soldiers, and this severe pedantic regularity, and the fact that all the trees were of the same size, and had tops and trunks all exactly alike, made them look monotonous and even dreary. Kovrin and Tanya walked along the rows where fires of dung, straw, and all sorts of refuse were smouldering, and from time to time they were met by labourers who wandered in the smoke like shadows. The only trees in flower were the cherries, plums, and certain sorts of apples, but the whole garden was plunged in smoke, and it was only near the nurseries that Kovrin could breathe freely.

'Even as a child I used to sneeze from the smoke here,' he said, shrugging his shoulders, 'but to this day I don't understand how smoke can keep off frost.'

'Smoke takes the place of clouds when there are none...' answered Tanya.

'And what do you want clouds for?'

'In overcast and cloudy weather there is no frost.'

'You don't say so.'

He laughed and took her arm. Her broad, very earnest face, chilled with the frost, with her delicate black eyebrows, the turned-up collar of her coat, which prevented her moving her head freely, and the whole of her thin, graceful figure, with her skirts tucked up on account of the dew, touched him.

'Good heavens! she is grown up,' he said. 'When I went away from here last, five years ago, you were still a child. You were such a thin, long-legged creature, with your hair hanging on your shoulders; you used to wear short frocks, and I used to tease you, calling you a heron... What time does!'

'Yes, five years!' sighed Tanya. 'Much water has flowed since then. Tell me, Andryusha, honestly,' she began eagerly, looking him in the face, 'do you feel strange with us now? But why do I ask you? You are a man, you live your own interesting life, you are somebody... To grow apart is so natural! But however that may be, Andryusha, I want you to think of us as your people. We have a right to that.'

'I do, Tanya.'

'On your word of honour?'

'Yes, on my word of honour.'

'You were surprised this evening that we have so many of your photographs. You know my father adores you. Sometimes it seems to me that he loves you more than he does me. He is proud of you. You are a clever, extraordinary man, you have made a brilliant career for yourself, and he is persuaded that you have turned out like this because he brought you up. I don't try to prevent him from thinking so. Let him.'

Dawn was already beginning, and that was especially perceptible from the distinctness with which the coils of smoke and the tops of the trees began to stand out in the air.

'It's time we were asleep, though,' said Tanya, 'and it's cold, too.' She took his arm. 'Thank you for coming, Andryusha. We have only uninteresting acquaintances, and not many of them. We have only the garden, the garden, the garden, and nothing else. Standards, half-standards,' she laughed. 'Aports, Reinettes, Borovinkas, budded stocks, grafted stocks... All, all our life has gone into the garden. I never even dream of anything but apples and pears. Of course, it is very nice and useful, but sometimes one longs for something else for variety. I remember that when you used to come to us for the summer holidays, or simply a visit, it always seemed to be fresher and brighter in the house, as though the covers had been taken off the lustres and the furniture. I was only a little girl then, but yet I understood it.'

She talked a long while and with great feeling. For some reason the idea came into his head that in the course of the summer he might grow fond of this little, weak, talkative creature, might be carried away and fall in love; in their position it was so possible and natural! This thought touched and amused him; he bent down to her sweet, preoccupied face and hummed softly:

"'Onyegin, I won't conceal it;
I madly love Tatiana...'"

By the time they reached the house, Yegor Semyonitch had got up.

Kovrin did not feel sleepy; he talked to the old man and went to the garden with him. Yegor Semyonitch was a tall, broad-shouldered, corpulent man, and he suffered from asthma, yet he walked so fast that it was hard work to hurry after him. He had an extremely preoccupied air; he was always hurrying somewhere, with an expression that suggested that if he were one minute late all would be ruined!

'Here is a business, brother...' he began, standing still to take breath. 'On the surface of the ground, as you see, is frost; but if you raise the thermometer on a stick fourteen feet above the ground, there it is warm...Why is that?'

'I really don't know,' said Kovrin, and he laughed.

'H'm!...One can't know everything, of course...However large the intellect may be, you can't find room for everything in it. I suppose you still go in chiefly for philosophy?'

'Yes, I lecture in psychology; I am working at philosophy in general.'

'And it does not bore you?'

'On the contrary, it's all I live for.'

'Well, God bless you!...' said Yegor Semyonitch, meditatively stroking his grey whiskers. 'God bless you!...I am delighted about you...delighted, my boy...'

But suddenly he listened, and, with a terrible face, ran off and quickly disappeared behind the trees in a cloud of smoke.

'Who tied this horse to an apple-tree?' Kovrin heard his despairing, heart-rending cry. 'Who is the low scoundrel who has dared to tie this horse to an apple-tree? My God, my God! They have ruined everything; they have spoilt everything; they have done everything filthy, horrible, and abominable. The orchard's done for, the orchard's ruined. My God!'

When he came back to Kovrin, his face looked exhausted and mortified.

'What is one to do with these accursed people?' he said in a tearful voice, flinging up his hands. 'Styopka was carting dung at night, and tied the horse to an apple-tree! He twisted the reins round it, the rascal, as tightly as he could, so that the bark is rubbed off in three places. What do you think of that! I spoke to him and he stands like a post and only blinks his eyes. Hanging is too good for him.'

Growing calmer, he embraced Kovrin and kissed him on the cheek.

'Well, God bless you!...God bless you!...' he muttered. 'I am very glad you have come. Unutterably glad...Thank you.'

Then, with the same rapid step and preoccupied face, he made the round of the whole garden, and showed his former ward all his greenhouses and hothouses, his covered-in garden, and two apiaries which he called the marvel of our century.

While they were walking the sun rose, flooding the garden with brilliant light. It grew warm. Foreseeing a long, bright, cheerful day, Kovrin recollected that it was only the beginning of May, and that he had before him a whole summer as bright, cheerful, and long; and suddenly there stirred in his bosom a joyous, youthful feeling, such as he used to experience in his childhood, running about in that garden. And he hugged the old man and kissed him affectionately. Both of them, feeling touched, went indoors and drank tea out of old-fashioned china cups, with cream and satisfying krendels made with milk and eggs; and these trifles reminded Kovrin again of his childhood and boyhood. The delightful present was blended with the impressions of the past that stirred within him; there was a tightness at his heart, yet he was happy.

He waited till Tanya was awake and had coffee with her, went for a walk, then went to his room and sat down to work. He read attentively, making notes, and from time to time raised his eyes to look out at the open windows or at the fresh, still dewy flowers in the vases on the table; and again he dropped his eyes to his book, and it seemed to him as though every vein in his body was quivering and fluttering with pleasure.

2

In the country he led just as nervous and restless a life as in town. He read and wrote a great deal, he studied Italian, and when he was out for a walk, thought with pleasure that he would soon sit down to work again. He slept so little that everyone wondered at him; if he accidentally dozed for half an hour in the daytime, he would lie awake all night, and, after a sleepless night, would feel cheerful and vigorous as though nothing had happened.

He walked a great deal, drank wine, and smoked expensive cigars. Very often, almost every day, young ladies of neighbouring families would come to the Pesotsky's, and would sing and play the piano with Tanya; sometimes a young neighbour who was a good violinist would come too. Kovrin listened with eagerness to the music and singing, and was exhausted by it, and this showed itself by his eyes closing and his head falling to one side.

One day he was sitting on the balcony after evening tea, reading. At the same time, in the drawing-room, Tanya taking soprano, one of the young ladies a contralto, and the young man with his violin, were practising a well-known serenade of Braga's. Kovrin listened to the words — they were Russian — and could not understand their meaning. At last, leaving his book and listening attentively, he understood: a maiden, full of sick fancies, heard one night in her garden mysterious sounds, so strange and lovely that she was obliged to recognize them as a holy harmony which is unintelligible to us mortals, and so flies back to heaven. Kovrin's eyes began to close. He got up, and in exhaustion walked up and down the drawing-room, and then the dining-room. When the singing was over he took Tanya's arm, and with her went out on to the balcony.

'I have been all day thinking of a legend,' he said. 'I don't remember whether I have read it somewhere or heard it, but it is a strange and almost grotesque legend. To begin with, it is somewhat obscure. A thousand years ago a monk, dressed in black, wandered about the desert, somewhere in Syria or Arabia.... Some miles from where he was, some fishermen saw another black monk, who was moving slowly over the surface of a lake. This second monk was a mirage. Now forget all the laws of optics, which the legend does not recognize, and listen to the rest. From that mirage there was cast another mirage, then from that other a third, so that the image of the black monk began to be repeated endlessly from one layer of the atmosphere to another. So that he was seen at one time in Africa, at another in Spain, then in Italy, then in the Far North.... Then he passed out of the atmosphere of the earth, and now he is wandering all over the universe, still never coming into conditions in which he might disappear. Possibly he may be seen now in Mars or in some star of the Southern Cross. But, my dear, the real point on which the whole legend hangs lies in the fact that, exactly a thousand years from the day when the monk walked in the desert, the mirage will return to the atmosphere of the earth again and will appear to men. And it seems that the thousand years is almost up.... According to the legend, we may look out for the black monk today or tomorrow.'

'A queer mirage,' said Tanya, who did not like the legend.

'But the most wonderful part of it all,' laughed Kovrin, 'is that I simply cannot recall where I got this legend from. Have I read it somewhere? Have I heard it? Or perhaps I dreamed of the black monk. I swear I don't remember. But the legend interests me. I have been thinking about it all day.'

Letting Tanya go back to her visitors, he went out of the house, and, lost in meditation, walked by the flower-beds. The sun was already setting. The flowers, having just been watered, gave forth a damp, irritating fragrance. Indoors they began singing again, and in the distance the violin had the effect of a human voice. Kovrin, racking his brains to remember where he had read or heard the legend, turned slowly towards the park, and unconsciously went as far as the river. By a little path that ran along the

... another black monk, who was moving slowly over the surface of a lake.

steep bank, between the bare roots, he went down to the water, disturbed the peewits there and frightened two ducks. The last rays of the setting sun still threw light here and there on the gloomy pines, but it was quite dark on the surface of the river. Kovrin crossed to the other side by the narrow bridge. Before him lay a wide field covered with young rye not yet in blossom. There was no living habitation, no living soul in the distance, and it seemed as though the little path, if one went along it, would take one to the unknown, mysterious place where the sun had just gone down, and where the evening glow was flaming in immensity and splendour.

'How open, how free, how still it is here!' thought Kovrin, walking along the path. 'And it feels as though all the world were watching me, hiding and waiting for me to understand it....'

But then waves began running across the rye, and a light evening breeze softly touched his uncovered head. A minute later there was another gust of wind, but stronger — the rye began rustling, and he heard behind him the hollow murmur of the pines. Kovrin stood still in amazement. From the horizon there rose up to the sky, like a whirlwind or a waterspout, a tall black column. Its outline was indistinct, but from the first instant it could be seen that it was not standing still, but moving with fearful rapidity, moving straight towards Kovrin, and the nearer it came the smaller and the more distinct it was. Kovrin moved aside into the rye to make way for it, and only just had time to do so.

A monk dressed in black with a grey head and black eyebrows, his arms crossed over his breast, floated by him.... His bare feet did not touch the earth. After he had floated twenty feet beyond him, he looked round at Kovrin, and nodded to him with a friendly but sly smile.

But what a pale, fearfully pale, thin face! Beginning to grow larger again, he flew across the river, collided noiselessly with the clay bank and pines, and passing through them, vanished like smoke.

'Why, you see,' muttered Kovrin, 'there must be truth in the legend.'

Without trying to explain to himself the strange apparition, glad that he had succeeded in seeing so near and so distinctly, not only the monk's black garments, but even his face and eyes, agreeably excited, he went back to the house.

In the park and in the garden people were moving about quietly, in the house they were playing — so he alone had seen the monk. He had an intense desire to tell Tanya and Yegor Semyonitch, but he reflected that they would certainly think his words the ravings of delirium, and that would frighten them; he had better say nothing.

He laughed aloud, sang, and danced the mazurka; he was in high spirits, and all of them, the visitors and Tanya, thought he had a peculiar look, radiant and inspired, and that he was very interesting.

3

After supper, when the visitors had gone, he went to his room and lay down on the sofa: he wanted to think about the monk. But a minute later Tanya came in.

'Here, Andryusha; read father's articles,' she said, giving him a bundle of pamphlets and proofs. 'They are splendid articles. He writes capitally.'

'Capitally, indeed!' said Yegor Semyonitch, following her and smiling constrainedly; he was ashamed. 'Don't listen to her, please; don't read them! Though, if you want to go to sleep, read them by all means; they are a fine soporific.'

'I think they are splendid articles,' said Tanya, with deep conviction. 'You read them, Andryusha, and persuade father to write oftener. He could write a complete manual of horticulture.'

Yegor Semyonitch gave a forced laugh, blushed, and began uttering the phrases usually made use of by an embarrassed author. At last he began to give way.

'In that case, begin with Gaucher's article and these Russian articles,' he muttered, turning over the pamphlets with a trembling hand, 'or else you won't understand. Before you read my objections, you must know what I am objecting to. But it's all nonsense...tiresome stuff. Besides, I believe it's bedtime.'

Tanya went away. Yegor Semyonitch sat down on the sofa by Kovrin and heaved a deep sigh.

'Yes, my boy...' he began after a pause. 'That's how it is, my dear lecturer. Here I write articles, and take part in exhibitions, and receive medals...Pesotsky, they say, has apples the size of a head, and Pesotsky, they say, has made his fortune with his garden. In short, "Kotcheby is rich and glorious". But one asks oneself: what is it all for? The garden is certainly fine, a model. It's not really a garden, but a regular institution, which is of the greatest public importance because it marks, so to say, a new era in Russian agriculture and Russian industry. But, what's it for? What's the object of it?'

'The fact speaks for itself.'

'I do not mean in that sense. I meant to ask: what will happen to the garden when I die? In the condition in which you see it now, it would not be maintained for one month without me. The whole secret of success lies not in its being a big garden or a great number of labourers being employed in it, but in the fact that I love the work. Do you understand? I love it perhaps more than myself. Look at me; I do everything myself. I work from morning to night: I do all the grafting myself, the pruning myself, the planting myself. I do it all myself: when anyone helps me I am jealous and irritable till I am rude. The whole secret lies in loving it — that is, in the sharp eye of the master; yes, and in the master's hands, and in the feeling that makes one, when one goes anywhere for an hour's visit, sit, ill at ease, with one's heart far away, afraid that something may have happened in the garden. But when I die, who will look after it? Who will work? The gardener? The labourers? Yes? But I tell you, my dear fellow, the worst enemy in the garden is not a hare, not a cockchafer, and not the frost, but any outside person.'

'And Tanya?' asked Kovrin, laughing. 'She can't be more harmful than a hare? She loves the work and understands it.'

'Yes, she loves it and understands it. If after my death the garden goes to her and she is the mistress, of course nothing better could be wished. But if, which God forbid, she should marry,' Yegor Semyonitch whispered, and looked with a frightened look at Kovrin, 'that's just it. If she marries and children come, she will have no time to think about the garden. What I fear most is: she will marry some fine gentleman, and he will be greedy, and he will let the garden to people who will run it for profit, and everything will go to the devil the very first year! In our work females are the scourge of God!'

Yegor Semyonitch sighed and paused for a while.

'Perhaps it is egoism, but I tell you frankly: I don't want Tanya to get married. I am afraid of it! There is one young dandy comes to see us, bringing his violin and scraping on it; I know Tanya will not marry him, I know it quite well; but I can't bear to see him! Altogether, my boy, I am very queer. I know that.'

Yegor Semyonitch got up and walked about the room in excitement, and it was evident that he wanted to say something very important, but could not bring himself to it.

'I am very fond of you, and so I am going to speak to you openly,' he decided at last, thrusting his hands into his pockets. 'I deal plainly with certain delicate questions, and say exactly what I think, and I cannot endure so-called hidden thoughts. I will speak plainly: you are the only man to whom I should not be afraid to marry my daughter. You are a clever man with a good heart, and would not let my beloved work go to ruin; and the

A. P. Chekhov

chief reason is that I love you as a son, and I am proud of you. If Tanya and you could get up a romance somehow, then — well! I should be very glad and even happy. I tell you this plainly, without mincing matters, like an honest man.'

Kovrin laughed. Yegor Semyonitch opened the door to go out, and stood in the doorway.

'If Tanya and you had a son, I would make a horticulturist of him,' he said, after a moment's thought. 'However, this is idle dreaming. Good night.'

Left alone, Kovrin settled himself more comfortably on the sofa and took up the articles. The title of one was 'On Intercropping'; of another, 'A Few Words on the Remarks of Monsieur Z. concerning the Trenching of the Soil for a New Garden'; a third, 'Additional Matter concerning Grafting with a Dormant Bud'; and they were all of the same sort. But what a restless, jerky tone! What nervous, almost hysterical passion! Here was an article, one would have thought, with most peaceable and impersonal contents: the subject of it was the Russian Antonovsky Apple. But Yegor Semyonitch began it with 'Audiatur altera pars,' and finished it with 'Sapienti sat'; and between these two quotations a perfect torrent of venomous phrases directed 'at the learned ignorance of our recognized horticultural authorities, who observe Nature from the height of their university chairs,' or at Monsieur Gaucher, 'whose success has been the work of the vulgar and the dilettanti.' And then followed an inappropriate, affected, and insincere regret that peasants who stole fruit and broke the branches could not nowadays be flogged.

'It is beautiful, charming, healthy work, but even in this there is strife and passion,' thought Kovrin. 'I suppose that everywhere and in all careers men of ideas are nervous, and marked by exaggerated sensitiveness. Most likely it must be so.'

He thought of Tanya, who was so pleased with Yegor Semyonitch's articles. Small, pale, and so thin that her shoulder-blades stuck out, her eyes, wide and open, dark and intelligent, had an intent gaze, as though looking for something. She walked like her father with a little hurried step. She talked a great deal and was fond of arguing, accompanying every phrase, however insignificant, with expressive mimicry and gesticulation. No doubt she was nervous in the extreme.

Kovrin went on reading the articles, but he understood nothing of them, and flung them aside. The same pleasant excitement with which he had earlier in the evening danced the mazurka and listened to the music was now mastering him again and rousing a multitude of thoughts. He got up and began walking about the room, thinking about the black monk. It occurred to him that if this strange, supernatural monk had appeared to him only, that meant that he was ill and had reached the point of having hallucinations.

This reflection frightened him, but not for long.

'But I am all right, and I am doing no harm to anyone; so there is no harm in my hallucinations,' he thought; and he felt happy again.

He sat down on the sofa and clasped his hands round his head. Restraining the unaccountable joy which filled his whole being, he then paced up and down again, and sat down to his work. But the thought that he read in the book did not satisfy him. He wanted something gigantic, unfathomable, stupendous. Towards morning he undressed and reluctantly went to bed: he ought to sleep.

When he heard the footsteps of Yegor Semyonitch going out into the garden, Kovrin rang the bell and asked the footman to bring him some wine. He drank several glasses of Lafitte, then wrapped himself up, head and all; his consciousness grew clouded and he fell asleep.

4

Yegor Semyonitch and Tanya often quarrelled and said nasty things to each other.

They quarrelled about something that morning. Tanya burst out crying and went to her room. She would not come down to dinner nor to tea. At first Yegor Semyonitch went about looking sulky and dignified, as though to give everyone to understand that for him the claims of justice and good order were more important than anything else in the world; but he could not keep it up for long, and soon sank into depression. He walked about the park dejectedly, continually sighing: 'Oh, my God! My God!' and at dinner did not eat a morsel. At last, guilty and conscience-stricken, he knocked at the locked door and called timidly:

'Tanya! Tanya!'

And from behind the door came a faint voice, weak with crying but still determined:

'Leave me alone, if you please.'

The depression of the master and mistress was reflected in the whole household, even in the labourers working in the garden. Kovrin was absorbed in his interesting work, but at last he, too, felt dreary and uncomfortable. To dissipate the general ill-humour in some way, he made up his mind to intervene, and towards evening he knocked at Tanya's door. He was admitted.

'Fie, fie, for shame!' he began playfully, looking with surprise at Tanya's tear-stained, woebegone face, flushed in patches with crying. 'Is it really so serious? Fie, fie!'

'But if you knew how he tortures me!' she said, and floods of scalding tears streamed from her big eyes. 'He torments me to death,' she went on, wringing her hands. 'I said nothing to him...nothing...I only said that there was no need to keep...too many labourers...if we could hire them by the day when we wanted nothing for a whole week. ... I ... I ... only said that, and he shouted and...said...a lot of horrible insulting things to me. What for?'

'There, there,' said Kovrin, smoothing her hair. 'You've quarrelled with each other, you've cried, and that's enough. You must not be angry for long — that's wrong — all the more as he loves you beyond everything.'

'He has...has spoiled my whole life,' Tanya went on, sobbing. 'I hear nothing but abuse and...insults. He thinks I am of no use in the house. Well! He is right. I shall go away tomorrow; I shall become a telegraph clerk. ... I don't care....'

'Come, come, come.... You mustn't cry, Tanya. You mustn't, dear.... You are both hot-tempered and irritable, and you are both to blame. Come along; I will reconcile you.'

Kovrin talked affectionately and persuasively, while she went on crying, twitching her shoulders and wringing her hands, as though some terrible misfortune had really befallen her. He felt all the sorrier for her because her grief was not a serious one, yet she suffered extremely. What trivialities were enough to make this little creature miserable for a whole day, perhaps for her whole life! Comforting Tanya, Kovrin thought that, apart from this girl and her father, he might hunt the world over and would not find people who would love him as one of themselves, as one of their kindred. If it had not been for those two he might very likely, having lost his father and mother in early childhood, never to the day of his death have known what was meant by genuine affection and that naive, uncritical love which is only lavished on very close blood relations; and he felt that the nerves of this weeping, shaking girl responded to his half-sick, overstrained nerves like iron to a magnet. He never could have loved a healthy, strong, rosy-cheeked woman, but pale, weak, unhappy Tanya attracted him.

And he liked stroking her hair and her shoulders, pressing her hand and wiping away her tears.... At last she left off crying. She went on for a long time complaining of her father and her hard, insufferable life in that house, entreating Kovrin to put himself in her place; then she began, little by little, smiling, and sighing that God had given her such a bad temper. At last, laughing aloud, she called herself a fool, and ran out of the room.

When a little later Kovrin went into the garden, Yegor Semyonitch and Tanya were walking side by side along an avenue as though nothing had happened, and both were eating rye bread with salt on it, as both were hungry.

5

Glad that he had been so successful in the part of peacemaker, Kovrin went into the park. Sitting on a garden seat, thinking, he heard the rattle of a carriage and a feminine laugh — visitors were arriving. When the shades of evening began falling on the garden, the sounds of the violin and singing voices reached him indistinctly, and that reminded him of the black monk. Where, in what land or in what planet, was that optical absurdity moving now?

Hardly had he recalled the legend and pictured in his imagination the dark apparition he had seen in the rye-field, when, from behind a pine-tree exactly opposite, there came out noiselessly, without the slightest rustle, a man of medium height with uncovered grey head, all in black, and barefooted like a beggar, and his black eyebrows stood out conspicuously on his pale, death-like face. Nodding his head graciously, this beggar or pilgrim came noiselessly to the seat and sat down, and Kovrin recognized him as the black monk.

For a minute they looked at one another, Kovrin with amazement, and the monk with friendliness, and, just as before, a little slyness, as though he were thinking something to himself.

'But you are a mirage,' said Kovrin. 'Why are you here and sitting still? That does not fit in with the legend.'

'That does not matter,' the monk answered in a low voice, not immediately turning his face towards him. 'The legend, the mirage, and I are all the products of your excited imagination. I am a phantom.'

'Then you don't exist?' said Kovrin.

'You can think as you like,' said the monk, with a faint smile. 'I exist in your imagination, and your imagination is part of nature, so I exist in nature.'

'You have a very old, wise, and extremely expressive face, as though you really had lived more than a thousand years,' said Kovrin. 'I did not

When the shades of evening began falling on the garden, the sounds of the violin...reached him indistinctly...

know that my imagination was capable of creating such phenomena. But why do you look at me with such enthusiasm? Do you like me?'

'Yes, you are one of those few who are justly called the chosen of God. You do the service of eternal truth. Your thoughts, your designs, the marvellous studies you are engaged in, and all your life, bear the Divine, the heavenly stamp, seeing that they are consecrated to the rational and the beautiful — that is, to what is eternal.'

'You said "eternal truth".... But is eternal truth of use to man and within his reach, if there is no eternal life?'

'There is eternal life,' said the monk.

'Do you believe in the immortality of man?'

'Yes, of course. A grand, brilliant future is in store for you men. And the more there are like you on earth, the sooner will this future be realized. Without you who serve the higher principle and live in full understanding and freedom, mankind would be of little account; developing in a natural way, it would have to wait a long time for the end of its earthly history. You will lead it some thousands of years earlier into the kingdom of eternal truth — and therein lies your supreme service. You are the incarnation of the blessing of God, which rests upon men.'

'And what is the object of eternal life?' asked Kovrin.

'As in all life — enjoyment. True enjoyment lies in knowledge, and eternal life provides innumerable and inexhaustible sources of knowledge, and in that sense it has been said: "In My Father's house there are many mansions".'

'If only you knew how pleasant it is to hear you!' said Kovrin, rubbing his hands with satisfaction.

'I am very glad.'

'But I know that when you go away I shall be worried by the question of your reality. You are a phantom, an hallucination. So I am mentally deranged, not normal?'

'What if you are? Why trouble yourself? You are ill because you have overworked and exhausted yourself, and that means that you have sacrificed your health to the idea, and the time is near at hand when you will give up life itself to it. What could be better? That is the goal towards which all divinely endowed, noble natures strive.'

'If I know I am mentally affected, can I trust myself?'

'And are you sure that the men of genius, whom all men trust, did not see phantoms, too? The learned say now that genius is allied to madness. My friend, healthy and normal people are not the common herd. Reflections upon the neurasthenia of the age, nervous exhaustion and degeneracy, etcetera, can only seriously agitate those who place the object of life in the present — that is, the common herd.'

'The Romans used to say: *Mens sana in corpore sano.*'

'Not everything the Greeks and Romans said is true. Exaltation, enthusiasm, ecstasy — all that distinguishes prophets, poets, martyrs for the idea, from the common folk — is repellent to the animal side of man — that is, his physical health. I repeat, if you want to be healthy and normal, go to the common herd.'

'Strange that you repeat what often comes into my mind,' said Kovrin. 'It is as though you had seen and overheard my secret thoughts. But don't let us talk about me. What do you mean by "eternal truth"?'

The monk did not answer. Kovrin looked at him and could not distinguish his face. His features grew blurred and misty. Then the monk's head and arms disappeared; his body seemed merged into the seat and the evening twilight, and he vanished altogether.

'The hallucination is over,' said Kovrin; and he laughed. 'It's a pity.'

He went back to the house, light-hearted and happy. The little the monk had said to him had flattered, not his vanity, but his whole soul, his whole being. To be one of the chosen, to serve eternal truth, to stand in the ranks of those who could make mankind worthy of the kingdom of God some thousands of years sooner — that is, to free men from some thousands of years of unnecessary struggle, sin, and suffering; to sacrifice to the idea everything — youth, strength, health; to be ready to die for the common weal — what an exalted, what a happy lot! He recalled his past — pure, chaste, laborious; he remembered what he had learned himself and what he had taught to others, and decided that there was no exaggeration in the monk's words.

Tanya came to meet him in the park: she was by now wearing a different dress.

'Are you here?' she said. 'And we have been looking and looking for you ... But what is the matter with you?' she asked in wonder, glancing at his radiant, ecstatic face and eyes full of tears. 'How strange you are, Andryusha!'

'I am pleased, Tanya,' said Kovrin, laying his hand on her shoulders. 'I am more than pleased: I am happy. Tanya, darling Tanya, you are an extraordinary, nice creature. Dear Tanya, I am so glad, I am so glad!'

He kissed both her hands ardently, and went on:

'I have just passed through an exalted, wonderful, unearthly moment. But I can't tell you all about it or you would call me mad and not believe me. Let us talk of you. Dear, delightful Tanya! I love you, and am used to loving you. To have you near me, to meet you a dozen times a day, has become a necessity of my existence; I don't know how I shall get on without you when I go back home.'

'Oh,' laughed Tanya, 'you will forget about us in two days. We are humble people and you are a great man.'

'No; let us talk in earnest!' he said. 'I shall take you with me, Tanya. Yes? Will you come with me? Will you be mine?'

'Come,' said Tanya, and tried to laugh again, but the laugh would not come, and patches of colour came into her face.

She began breathing quickly and walked very quickly, but not to the house, but further into the park.

'I was not thinking of it...I was not thinking of it,' she said, wringing her hands in despair.

And Kovrin followed her and went on talking, with the same radiant, enthusiastic face:

'I want a love that will dominate me altogether; and that love only you, Tanya, can give me. I am happy! I am happy!'

She was overwhelmed, and huddling and shrinking together, seemed ten years older all at once, while he thought her beautiful and expressed his rapture aloud:

'How lovely she is!'

6

Learning from Kovrin that not only a romance had been got up, but that there would even be a wedding, Yegor Semyonitch spent a long time in pacing from one corner of the room to the other, trying to conceal his agitation. His hands began trembling, his neck swelled and turned purple, he ordered his racing droshky and drove off somewhere. Tanya, seeing how he lashed the horse, and seeing how he pulled his cap over his ears, understood what he was feeling, shut herself up in her room, and cried the whole day.

In the hothouses the peaches and plums were already ripe; the packing and sending off of these tender and fragile goods to Moscow took a great deal of care, work, and trouble. Owing to the fact that the summer was very hot and dry, it was necessary to water every tree, and a great deal of time and labour was spent on doing it. Numbers of caterpillars made their appearance, which, to Kovrin's disgust, the labourers and even Yegor Semyonitch and Tanya squashed with their fingers. In spite of all that, they had already to book autumn orders for fruit and trees, and to carry on a great deal of correspondence. And at the very busiest time, when no one seemed to have a free moment, the work of the fields carried off more than half their labourers from the garden. Yegor Semyonitch, sunburnt, exhausted, ill-humoured, galloped from the fields to the garden and back again; cried that he was being torn to pieces, and that he should put a bullet through his brains.

Numbers of caterpillars made their appearance, which ... the labourers ... squashed with their fingers.

Then came the fuss and worry of the trousseau, to which the Pesotskys attached a good deal of importance. Everyone's head was in a whirl from the snipping of the scissors, the rattle of the sewing-machine, the smell of hot irons, and the caprices of the dressmaker, a huffy and nervous lady. And, as ill-luck would have it, visitors came every day, who had to be entertained, fed, and even put up for the night. But all this hard labour passed unnoticed as though in a fog. Tanya felt that love and happiness had taken her unawares, though she had, since she was fourteen, for some reason been convinced that Kovrin would marry her and no one else. She was bewildered, could not grasp it, could not believe herself... At one minute such joy would swoop down upon her that she longed to fly away to the clouds and there pray to God, at another moment she would remember that in August she would have to part from her home and leave her father; or, goodness knows why, the idea would occur to her that she was worthless – insignificant and unworthy of a great man like Kovrin – and she would go to her room, lock herself in, and cry bitterly for several hours. When there were visitors, she would suddenly fancy that Kovrin looked extraordinarily handsome, and that all the women were in love with him and envying her, and her soul was filled with pride and rapture, as though she had vanquished the whole world; but he had only to smile politely at any young lady for her to be trembling with jealousy, to retreat to her room – and tears again. These new sensations mastered her completely; she helped her father mechanically, without noticing peaches, caterpillars or labourers, or how rapidly the time was passing.

It was almost the same with Yegor Semyonitch. He worked from morning till night, was always in a hurry, was irritable, and flew into rages, but all of this was in a sort of spellbound dream. It seemed as though there were two men in him: one was the real Yegor Semyonitch, who was moved to indignation, and clutched his head in despair when he heard of some irregularity from Ivan Karlovitch the gardener; and another – not the real one – who seemed as though he were half drunk, would interrupt a business conversation at half a word, touch the gardener on the shoulder, and begin muttering:

'Say what you like, there is a great deal in blood. His mother was a wonderful woman, most high-minded and intelligent. It was a pleasure to look at her good, candid, pure face; it was like the face of an angel. She drew splendidly, wrote verses, spoke five foreign languages, sang.... Poor thing! she died of consumption. The Kingdom of Heaven be hers.'

The unreal Yegor Semyonitch sighed, and after a pause went on: 'When he was a boy and growing up in my house, he had the same angelic face, good and candid. The way he looks and talks and moves is as soft and elegant as his mother's. And his intellect! We were always struck with his intelligence. To be sure, it's not for nothing he's a Master of Arts! It's not for nothing! And wait a bit, Ivan Karlovitch, what will he be in ten years' time? He will be far above us!'

But at this point the real Yegor Semyonitch, suddenly coming to himself, would make a terrible face, would clutch his head and cry:

'The devils! They have spoilt everything! They have ruined everything! They have spoilt everything! The garden's done for, the garden's ruined!'

Kovrin, meanwhile, worked with the same ardour as before, and did not notice the general commotion. Love only added fuel to the flames. After every talk with Tanya he went to his room, happy and triumphant, took up his book or his manuscript with the same passion with which he had just kissed Tanya, and told her of his love. What the black monk had told him of the chosen of God, of eternal truth, of the brilliant future of mankind and so on, gave peculiar and extraordinary significance to his work, and filled his soul with pride and the consciousness of his own exalted consequence. Once or twice a week, in the park or in the house, he met the black monk and had long conversations with him, but this did not alarm him, but, on the contrary, delighted him, as he was now firmly persuaded that such apparitions only visited the elect few who rise up above their fellows and devote themselves to the service of the idea.

One day the monk appeared at dinner-time and sat in the dining-room window. Kovrin was delighted, and very adroitly began a conversation with Yegor Semyonitch and Tanya of what might be of interest to the monk; the black-robed visitor listened and nodded his head graciously, and Yegor Semyonitch and Tanya listened, too, and smiled gaily without suspecting that Kovrin was not talking to them but to his hallucination.

Imperceptibly the feast of the Assumption was approaching, and soon after came the wedding, which, at Yegor Semyonitch's urgent desire, was celebrated with "a flourish" — that is, with senseless festivities that lasted for two whole days and nights. Three thousand roubles' worth of food and drink was consumed, but the music of the wretched hired band, the noisy toasts, the scurrying to and fro of the footmen, the uproar and crowding, prevented them from approaching the taste of the expensive wines and wonderful delicacies ordered from Moscow.

7

One long winter night Kovrin was lying in bed, reading a French novel. Poor Tanya, who had headaches in the evenings from living in town, to which she was not accustomed, had been asleep a long while, and, from time to time, articulated some incoherent phrase in her restless dreams.

It struck three o'clock. Kovrin put out the light and lay down to sleep, lay for a long time with his eyes closed, but could not get to sleep because, as he fancied, the room was very hot and Tanya talked in her sleep. At half-past four he lighted the candle again, and this time he saw the black monk sitting in an arm-chair near the bed.

'Good morning,' said the monk, and after a brief pause he asked: 'What are you thinking of now?'

'Of fame,' answered Kovrin. 'In the French novel I have just been reading, there is a description of a young *savant*, who does silly things and pines away through worrying about fame. I can't understand such anxiety.'

'Because you are wise. Your attitude towards fame is one of indifference, as towards a toy which no longer interests you.'

'Yes, that is true.'

'Renown does not allure you now. What is there flattering, amusing, or edifying in their carving your name on a tombstone, then time rubbing off the inscription together with the gilding? Moreover, happily there are too many of you for the weak memory of mankind to be able to retain your names.'

'Of course,' assented Kovrin. 'Besides, why whould they be remembered? But let us talk of something else. Of happiness, for instance. What is happiness?'

When the clock struck five, he was sitting on the bed, dangling his feet to the carpet, talking to the monk:

'In ancient times a happy man grew at last frightened of his happiness − it was so great! − and to propitiate the gods he brought as a sacrifice his favourite ring. Do you know, I, too, like Polykrates, begin to be uneasy of my happiness. It seems strange to me that from morning to night I feel nothing but joy; it fills my whole being and smothers all other feelings. I don't know what sadness, grief, or boredom is. Here I am not asleep; I suffer from sleeplessness, but I am not dull. I say it in earnest; I begin to feel perplexed.'

'But why?' the monk asked in wonder. 'Is joy a supernatural feeling? Ought it not to be the normal state of man? The more highly a man is developed on the intellectual and moral side, the more independent he is, the more pleasure life gives him. Socrates, Diogenes, and Marcus Aurelius were joyful, not sorrowful. And the Apostle tells us: "Rejoice continually"; "Rejoice and be glad."'

'But will the gods be suddenly wrathful?' Kovrin jested; and he laughed. 'If they take from me comfort and make me go cold and hungry, it won't be very much to my taste.'

Meanwhile Tanya woke up, and looked with amazement and horror at her husband. He was talking, addressing the arm-chair, laughing and gesticulating; his eyes were gleaming, and there was something strange in his laugh.

'Andryusha, whom are you talking to?' she asked, clutching the hand he stretched out to the monk. 'Andryusha! Whom?'

'Oh! Whom?' said Kovrin in confusion. 'Why, to him... He is sitting here,' he said, pointing to the black monk.

'There is no one here... no one! Andryusha, you are ill!'

Tanya put her arm round her husband and held him tight, as though protecting him from the apparition, and put her hand over his eyes.

'You are ill!' she sobbed, trembling all over. 'Forgive me, my precious, my dear one, but I have noticed for a long time that your mind is clouded in some way... You are mentally ill, Andryusha...'

Her trembling infected him, too. He glanced once more at the arm-chair, which was now empty, felt a sudden weakness in his arms and legs, was frightened, and began dressing.

'It's nothing, Tanya; it's nothing,' he muttered, shivering. 'I really am not quite well...it's time to admit that.'

'I have noticed it for a long time...and father has noticed it,' she said, trying to suppress her sobs. 'You talk to yourself, smile somehow strangely...and can't sleep. Oh, my God, my God, save us!' she said in terror. 'But don't be frightened, Andryusha; for God's sake don't be frightened...'

She began dressing, too. Only now, looking at her, Kovrin realized the danger of his position − realized the meaning of the black monk and his conversations with him. It was clear to him now that he was mad.

Neither of them knew why they dressed and went into the dining-room: she in front and he following her. There they found Yegor Semyonitch standing in his dressing-gown and with a candle in his hand. He was staying with them, and had been awakened by Tanya's sobs.

'Don't be frightened, Andryusha,' Tanya was saying, shivering as though in a fever; 'don't be frightened... Father, it will all pass over...it will all pass over...'

Kovrin was too much agitated to speak. He wanted to say to his father-in-law in a playful tone: 'Congratulate me; it appears I have gone out of my mind'; but he could only move his lips and smile bitterly.

At nine o'clock in the morning they put on his jacket and fur coat, wrapped him up in a shawl, and took him in a carriage to a doctor.

8

Summer had come again, and the doctor advised their going into the

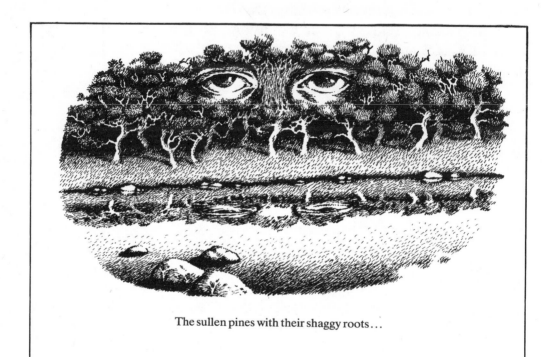

The sullen pines with their shaggy roots…

country. Kovrin had recovered; he had left off seeing the black monk, and he had only to get up his strength. Staying at his father-in-law's, he drank a great deal of milk, worked for only two hours out of the twenty-four, and neither smoked nor drank wine.

On the evening before Elijah's Day they had an evening service in the house. When the deacon was handing the priest the censer the immense old room smelt like a graveyard, and Kovrin felt bored. He went out into the garden. Without noticing the gorgeous flowers, he walked about the garden, sat down on a seat, then strolled about the park; reaching the river, he went down and then stood lost in thought, looking at the water. The sullen pines with their shaggy roots, which had seen him a year before so young, so joyful and confident, were not whispering now, but standing mute and motionless, as though they did not recognize him. And, indeed, his head was closely cropped, his beautiful long hair was gone, his step was lagging, his face was fuller and paler than last summer.

He crossed by the footbridge to the other side. Where the year before there had been rye the oats stood, reaped, and lay in rows. The sun had set and there was a broad stretch of glowing red on the horizon, a sign of windy weather next day. It was still. Looking in the direction from which the year before the black monk had first appeared, Kovrin stood for twenty minutes, till the evening glow had begun to fade....

When, listless and dissatisfied, he returned home the service was over. Yegor Semyonitch and Tanya were sitting on the steps of the verandah, drinking tea. They were talking of something, but, seeing Kovrin, ceased at once, and he concluded from their faces that their talk had been about him.

'I believe it is time for you to have your milk,' Tanya said to her husband.

'No, it is not time yet...' he said, sitting down on the bottom step. 'Drink it yourself; I don't want it.'

Tanya exchanged a troubled glance with her father, and said in a guilty voice:

'You notice yourself that milk does you good.'

'Yes, a great deal of good!' Kovrin laughed. 'I congratulate you: I have gained a pound in weight since Friday.' He pressed his head tightly in his hands and said miserably: 'Why, why have you cured me? Preparations of bromide, idleness, hot baths, supervision, cowardly consternation at every mouthful, at every step — all this will reduce me at last to idiocy. I went out of my mind, I had megalomania; but then I was cheerful, confident, and even happy; I was interesting and original. Now I have become more sensible and stolid, but I am just like everyone else: I am — mediocrity; I am weary of life.... Oh, how cruelly you have treated me!...I saw hallucinations, but what harm did that do to anyone? I ask, what harm did that do anyone?'

'Goodness knows what you are saying!' sighed Yegor Semyonitch. 'It's positively wearisome to listen to it.'

'Then don't listen.'

The presence of other people, especially Yegor Semyonitch, irritated Kovrin now; he answered him drily, coldly, and even rudely, never looked at him but with irony and hatred, while Yegor Semyonitch was overcome with confusion and cleared his throat guiltily, though he was not conscious of any fault in himself. At a loss to understand why their charming and affectionate relations had changed so abruptly, Tanya huddled up to her father and looked anxiously in his face; she wanted to understand and could not understand, and all that was clear to her was that their relations were growing worse and worse every day, that of late her father had begun to look much older, and her husband had grown irritable, capricious, quarrelsome and uninteresting. She could not laugh or sing; at dinner she ate nothing; did not sleep for nights together, expecting something awful, and was so worn out that on one occasion she lay in a dead faint from dinner-time till evening. During the service she thought her father was crying, and now while the three of them were sitting together on the terrace she made an effort not to think of it.

'How fortunate Buddha, Mahomed, and Shakespeare were that their kind relations and doctors did not cure them of their ecstasy and their inspiration,' said Kovrin. 'If Mahomed had taken bromide for his nerves, had worked only two hours out of the twenty-four, and had drunk milk, that remarkable man would have left no more trace after him than his dog. Doctors and kind relations will succeed in stupefying mankind, in making mediocrity pass for genius and in bringing civilization to ruin. If only you knew,' Kovrin said with annoyance, 'how grateful I am to you.'

He felt intense irritation, and to avoid saying too much, he got up quickly and went into the house. It was still, and the fragrance of the tobacco plant and the marvel of Peru floated in at the open window. The moonlight lay in green patches on the floor and on the piano in the big dark dining-room. Kovrin remembered the raptures of the previous summer when there had been the same scent of the marvel of Peru and the moon had shone in at the window. To bring back the moon of last year he went quickly to his study, lighted a strong cigar, and sent the footman to bring him some wine. But the cigar left a bitter and disgusting taste in his mouth, and the wine had not the same flavour as it had the year before. And so great is the effect of giving up a habit, the cigar and the two gulps of wine made him giddy, and brought on palpitations of the heart, so that he was obliged to take bromide.

Before going to bed, Tanya said to him:

A. P. Chekhov

'Father adores you. You are cross with him about something, and it is killing him. Look at him; he is ageing, not from day to day, but from hour to hour. I entreat you, Andryusha, for God's sake, for the sake of your dead father, for the sake of my peace of mind, be affectionate to him.'

'I can't, I don't want to.'

'But why?' asked Tanya, beginning to tremble all over. 'Explain why.'

'Because he is antipathetic to me, that's all,' said Kovrin carelessly; and he shrugged his shoulders. 'But we won't talk about him: he is your father.'

'I can't understand, I can't,' said Tanya, pressing her hands to her temples and staring at a fixed point. 'Something incomprehensible, awful, is going on in the house. You have changed, grown unlike yourself.... You, clever, extraordinary man as you are, are irritated over trifles, meddle in paltry nonsense.... Such trivial things excite you, that sometimes one is simply amazed and can't believe that it is you. Come, come, don't be angry, don't be angry,' she went on, kissing his hands, frightened of her own words. 'You are clever, kind, noble. You will be just to father. He is so good.'

'He is not good; he is just good-natured. Burlesque old uncles like your father, with well-fed, good-natured faces, extraordinarily hospitable and queer, at one time used to touch me and amuse me in novels and in farces and in life; now I dislike them. They are egoists to the marrow of their bones. What disgusts me most of all is their being so well-fed, and that purely bovine, purely hoggish optimism of a full stomach.'

Tanya sat down on the bed and laid her head on the pillow.

'This is torture,' she said, and from her voice it was evident that she was utterly exhausted, and that it was hard for her to speak. 'Not one moment of peace since the winter.... Why, it's awful! My God! I am wretched.'

'Oh, of course, I am Herod, and you and your father are the innocents. Of course.'

His face seemed to Tanya ugly and unpleasant. Hatred and an ironical expression did not suit him. And, indeed, she had noticed before that there was something lacking in his face, as though ever since his hair had been cut his face had changed, too. She wanted to say something wounding to him, but immediately she caught herself in this antagonistic feeling, she was frightened and went out of the bedroom.

9

Kovrin received a professorship at the University. The inaugural address was fixed for the second of December, and a notice to that effect was hung up in the corridor at the University. But on the day appointed he informed the students' inspector, by telegram, that he was prevented by illness from giving the lecture.

He had hæmorrhage from the throat. He was often spitting blood, but it happened two or three times a month that there was a considerable loss of blood, and then he grew extremely weak and sank into a drowsy condition. This illness did not particularly frighten him, as he knew that his mother had lived for ten years or longer suffering from the same disease, and the doctors assured him that there was no danger, and had only advised him to avoid excitement, to lead a regular life, and to speak as little as possible.

In January again his lecture did not take place owing to the same reason, and in February it was too late to begin the course. It had to be postponed to the following year.

By now he was living not with Tanya, but with another woman, who was two years older than he was, and who looked after him as though he were a baby. He was in a calm and tranquil state of mind; he readily gave in to her, and when Varvara Nikolaevna — that was the name of his friend — decided to take him to the Crimea, he agreed, though he had a presentiment that no good would come of the trip.

They reached Sevastopol in the evening and stopped at an hotel to rest and go on the next day to Yalta. They were both exhausted by the journey. Varvara Nikolaevna had some tea, went to bed and was soon asleep. But Kovrin did not go to bed. An hour before starting for the station, he had received a letter from Tanya, and had not brought himself to open it, and now it was lying in his coat pocket, and the thought of it excited him disagreeably. At the bottom of his heart he genuinely considered now that his marriage to Tanya had been a mistake. He was glad that their separation was final, and the thought of that woman who in the end had turned into a living relic, still walking about though everything seemed dead in her except her big, staring, intelligent eyes — the thought of her roused in him nothing but pity and disgust with himself. The hand-writing on the envelope reminded him how cruel and unjust he had been two years before, how he had worked off his anger at his spiritual emptiness, his boredom, his loneliness, and his dissatisfaction with life by revenging himself on people in no way to blame. He remembered, also, how he had torn up his dissertation and all the articles he had written during his illness, and how he had thrown them out of the window, and the bits of paper had fluttered in the wind and caught on the trees and flowers. In every line of them he saw strange, utterly groundless pretension, shallow defiance, arrogance, megalomania; and they made him feel as though he were reading a description of his vices. But when the last manuscript had been torn up and sent flying out of the window, he felt, for some reason, suddenly bitter and angry; he went to his wife and said a great many unpleasant things to her. My God, how he had tormented her! One day, wanting to cause her pain, he told her that her father had played a very unattractive part in their romance, that he had asked him to marry her. Yegor Semyonitch accidentally overheard this, ran into the room, and, in his despair, could not utter a word, could only stamp and make a strange, bellowing sound as though he had lost the power of speech, and Tanya, looking at her father, had uttered a heart-rending shriek and had fallen into a swoon. It was hideous.

All this came back to his memory as he looked at the familiar writing. Kovrin went out on to the balcony; it was still warm weather and there was a smell of the sea. The wonderful bay reflected the moonshine and the lights, and was of a colour for which it was difficult to find a name. It was a soft and tender blending of dark blue and green; in places the water was like blue vitriol, and in places it seemed as though the moonlight were liquefied and filling the bay instead of water. And what harmony of colours, what an atmosphere of peace, calm, and sublimity!

In the lower storey under the balcony the windows were probably open, for women's voices and laughter could be heard distinctly. Apparently there was an evening party.

Kovrin made an effort, tore open the envelope, and, going back into his room, read:

'My father is just dead. I owe that to you, for you have killed him. Our garden is being ruined; strangers are managing it already — that is, the very thing is happening that poor father dreaded. That too, I owe to you. I hate you with my whole soul, and I hope you may soon perish. Oh, how wretched I am! Insufferable anguish is burning my soul.... My curses on you. I took you for an extraordinary man, a genius; I loved you, and you have turned out a madman....'

Kovrin could read no more, he tore up the letter and threw it away. He was overcome by an uneasiness that was akin to terror. Varvara Nikolaevna was asleep behind the screen, and he could hear her breathing. From the lower storey came the sounds of laughter and women's voices, but he felt as though in the whole hotel there were no living soul but him. Because Tanya, unhappy, broken by sorrow, had cursed him in her letter and hoped for his perdition, he felt eerie and kept glancing hurriedly at the door, as though he were afraid that the uncomprehended force which two years before had

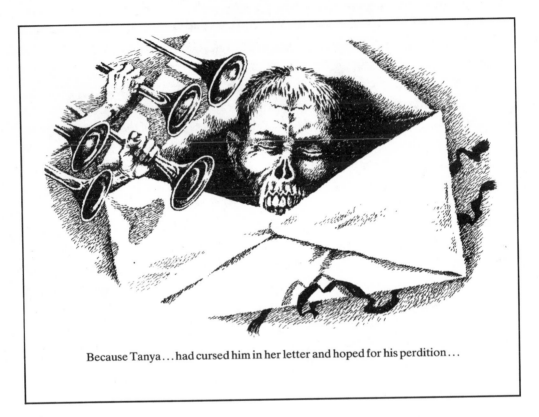

Because Tanya... had cursed him in her letter and hoped for his perdition...

wrought such havoc in his life and in the life of those near him might come into the room and master him once more.

He knew by experience that when his nerves were out of hand the best thing for him to do was to work. He must sit down to the table and force himself, at all costs, to concentrate his mind on some one thought. He took from his red portfolio a manuscript containing a sketch of a small work of the nature of a compilation, which he had planned in case he should find it dull in the Crimea without work. He sat down to the table and began working at this plan, and it seemed to him that his calm, peaceful, indifferent mood was coming back. The manuscript with the sketch even led him to meditation on the vanity of the world. He thought how much life exacts for the worthless or very commonplace blessings it can give a man. For instance, to gain, before forty, a university chair, to be an ordinary professor, to expound ordinary and second-hand thoughts in dull, heavy, insipid language — in fact, to gain the position of a mediocre learned man, he, Kovrin, had had to study for fifteen years, to work day and night, to endure a terrible mental illness, to experience an unhappy marriage, and to do a great number of stupid and unjust things which it would have been pleasant not to remember. Kovrin recognized clearly, now, that he was a mediocrity, and readily resigned himself to it, as he considered that every man ought to be satisfied with what he is.

The plan of the volume would have soothed him completely, but the torn letter showed white on the floor and prevented him from concentrating his attention. He got up from the table, picked up the pieces of the letter and threw them out of the window, but there was a light wind blowing from the sea, and the bits of paper were scattered on the window-sill. Again he was overcome by uneasiness akin to terror, and he felt as though in the whole hotel there were no living soul but himself.... He went out on the balcony. The bay, like a living thing, looked at him with its multitude of light blue, dark blue, turquoise and fiery eyes, and seemed beckoning to him. And it really was hot and oppressive, and it would not have been amiss to have to bathe.

Suddenly in the lower storey under the balcony a violin began playing, and two soft feminine voices began singing. It was something familiar. The song was about a maiden, full of sick fancies, who heard one night in her garden mysterious sounds, so strange and lovely that she was obliged to recognize them as a holy harmony which is unintelligible to us mortals, and so flies back to heaven.... Kovrin caught his breath and there was a pang of sadness at his heart, and a thrill of the sweet, exquisite delight he had so long forgotten began to stir in his breast.

A tall black column, like a whirlwind or a waterspout, appeared on the further side of the bay. It moved with fearful rapidity across the bay, towards the hotel, growing smaller and darker as it came, and Kovrin only just had time to get out of the way to let it pass.... The monk with bare grey head, black eyebrows, barefoot, his arms crossed over his breast, floated by him, and stood still in the middle of the room.

'Why did you not believe me?' he asked reproachfully, looking affectionately at Kovrin. 'If you had believed me then, that you were a genius, you would not have spent these two years so gloomily and so wretchedly.'

Kovrin already believed that he was one of God's chosen and a genius; he vividly recalled his conversations with the monk in the past and tried to speak, but the blood flowed from his throat on to his breast, and not knowing what he was doing, he passed his hands over his breast, and his cuffs were soaked with blood. He tried to call Varvara Nikolaevna, who was asleep behind the screen, he made an effort and said:

'Tanya!'

He fell on the floor, and propping himself on his arms, called again:

'Tanya!'

He called Tanya, called to the great garden with the gorgeous flowers sprinkled with dew, called to the park, the pines with their shaggy roots, the rye-field, his marvellous learning, his youth, courage, joy — called to life, which was so lovely. He saw on the floor near his face a great pool of blood, and was too weak to utter a word, but an unspeakable, infinite happiness flooded his whole being. Below, under the balcony, they were playing the serenade, and the black monk whispered to him that he was a genius, and that he was dying only because his frail human body had lost its balance and could no longer serve as the mortal garb of genius.

When Varvara Nikolaevna woke up and came out from behind the screen, Kovrin was dead, and a blissful smile was set upon his face.

Sir Arthur Conan Doyle
SELECTING A GHOST

I AM sure that Nature never intended me to be a self-made man. There are times when I can hardly bring myself to realize that twenty years of my life were spent behind the counter of a grocer's shop in the East End of London, and that it was through such an avenue that I reached a wealthy independence and the possession of Goresthorpe Grange. My habits are conservative; and my tastes refined and aristocratic. I have a soul which spurns the vulgar herd. Our family, the D'Odds, date back to a prehistoric era, as is to be inferred from the fact that their advent into British history is not commented on by any trustworthy historian. Some instinct tells me that the blood of a Crusader runs in my veins. Even now, after the lapse of so many years, such exclamations as 'By'r Lady!' rise naturally to my lips, and I feel that, should circumstances require it, I am capable of rising in my stirrups and dealing an infidel a blow — say with a mace — which would considerably astonish him.

Goresthorpe Grange is a feudal mansion — or so it was termed in the advertisement which originally brought it under my notice. Its right to this adjective had a most remarkable effect upon its price, and the advantages gained may possibly be more sentimental than real. Still, it is soothing to me to know that I have slits in my staircase through which I can discharge arrows; and there is a sense of power in the fact of possessing a complicated apparatus by means of which I am enabled to pour molten lead upon the head of the casual visitor. These things chime in with my peculiar humour, and I do not grudge to pay for them. I am proud of my battlements and of the circular uncovered sewer which girds me round. I am proud of my portcullis and donjon and keep. There is but one thing wanting to round off the mediaevalism of my abode, and to render it symmetrically and completely antique. Goresthorpe Grange is not provided with a ghost.

Any man with old-fashioned tastes and ideas as to how such establishments should be conducted would have been disappointed at the omission. In my case it was particularly unfortunate. From my childhood I had been an earnest student of the supernatural, and a firm believer in it. I have revelled in ghostly literature until there is hardly a tale bearing upon the subject which I have not perused. I learned the German language for the sole purpose of mastering a book upon demonology. When an infant I have secreted myself in dark rooms in the hope of seeing some of those bogies with which my nurse used to threaten me; and the same feeling is as strong in me now as then. It was a proud moment when I felt that a ghost was one of the luxuries which my money might command.

It is true that there was no mention of an apparition in the advertisement. On reviewing the mildewed walls, however, and the shadowy corridors, I had taken it for granted that there was such a thing on the premises. As the presence of a kennel presupposes that of a dog, so I imagined that it was impossible that such desirable quarters should be untenanted by one or more restless shades. Good heavens, what can the noble family from whom I purchased it have been doing during these

My habits are conservative; and my tastes refined and aristocratic.

hundreds of years! Was there no member of it spirited enough to make away with his sweetheart, or take some other steps calculated to establish a hereditary spectre? Even now I can hardly write with patience upon the subject.

For a long time I hoped against hope. Never did a rat squeak behind the wainscot, or rain drip upon the attic-floor, without a wild thrill shooting through me as I thought that at last I had come upon traces of some unquiet soul. I felt no touch of fear upon these occasions. If it occurred in the night-time, I would send Mrs D'Odd — who is a strong-minded woman — to investigate the matter while I covered up my head with the bedclothes and indulged in an ecstasy of expectation. Alas, the result was always the same! The suspicious sound would be traced to some cause so absurdly natural and commonplace that the most fervid imagination could not clothe it with any of the glamour of romance.

I might have reconciled myself to this state of things had it not been for Jorrocks of Havistock Farm. Jorrocks is a coarse, burly, matter-of-fact fellow, whom I only happen to know through the accidental circumstance of his fields adjoining my demesne. Yet this man, though utterly devoid of all appreciation of archaeological unities, is in possession of a well-authenti-cated and undeniable spectre. Its existence only dates back, I believe, to the reign of the Second George, when a young lady cut her throat upon hearing of the death of her lover at the battle of Dettingen. Still, even that gives the house an air of respectability, especially when coupled with bloodstains upon the floor. Jorrocks is densely unconscious of his good fortune; and his language when he reverts to the apparition is painful to listen to. He little dreams how I covet every one of those moans and nocturnal wails which he describes with unnecessary objurgation. Things are indeed coming to a pretty pass when democratic spectres are allowed to desert the landed proprietors and annul every social distinction by taking refuge in the houses of the great unrecognized.

I have a large amount of perseverance. Nothing else could have raised me into my rightful sphere, considering the uncongenial atmosphere in which I spent the earlier part of my life. I felt now that a ghost must be secured, but how to set about securing one was more than either Mrs D'Odd or myself was able to determine. My reading taught me that such phenomena are usually the outcome of crime. What crime was to be done, then, and who was to do it? A wild idea entered my mind that Watkins, the house-steward, might be prevailed upon − for a consideration − to immolate himself or someone else in the interests of the establishment. I put the matter to him in a half-jesting manner; but it did not seem to strike him in a favourable light. The other servants sympathized with him in his opinion− at least, I cannot account in any other way for their having left the house in a body the same afternoon.

'My dear,' Mrs D'Odd remarked to me one day after dinner, as I sat moodily sipping a cup of sack − I love the good old names − 'my dear, that odious ghost of Jorrocks' has been gibbering again.'

'Let it gibber!' I answered recklessly.

Mrs D'Odd struck a few chords on her virginal and looked thoughtfully into the fire.

'I'll tell you what it is, Argentine,' she said at last, using the pet name which we usually substituted for Silas, 'we must have a ghost sent down from London.'

'How can you be so idiotic, Matilda?' I remarked severely. 'Who could get us such a thing?'

'My cousin, Jack Brocket, could,' she answered confidently.

Now, this cousin of Matilda's was rather a sore subject between us. He was a rakish clever young fellow, who had tried his hand at many things, but wanted perseverance to succeed at any. He was, at that time, in chambers in London, professing to be a general agent, and really living, to a great extent, upon his wits. Matilda managed so that most of our business should pass through his hands, which certainly saved me a great deal of trouble; but I found that Jack's commission was generally considerably larger than all the other items of the bill put together. It was this fact which made me feel inclined to rebel against any further negotiations with the young gentleman.

'O yes, he could,' insisted Mrs D., seeing the look of disapprobation upon my face. 'You remember how well he managed that business about the crest?'

'It was only a resuscitation of the old family coat-of-arms, my dear,' I protested.

Matilda smiled in an irritating manner. 'There was a resuscitation of the family portraits, too, dear,' she remarked. 'You must allow that Jack selected them very judiciously.'

I thought of the long line of faces which adorned the walls of my banqueting-hall, from the burly Norman robber, through every gradation of casque, plume, and ruff, to the sombre Chesterfieldian individual who appears to have staggered against a pillar in his agony at the return of a maiden manuscript which he grips convulsively in his right hand. I was fain to confess that in that instance he had done his work well, and that it was only fair to give him an order – with the usual commission – for a family spectre, should such a thing be attainable.

It is one of my maxims to act promptly when once my mind is made up. Noon of the next day found me ascending the spiral stone staircase which leads to Mr Brocket's chambers, and admiring the succession of arrows and fingers upon the whitewashed wall, all indicating the direction of that gentleman's sanctum. As it happened, artificial aids of the sort were entirely unnecessary, as an animated flap-dance overhead could proceed from no other quarter, though it was replaced by a deathly silence as I groped my way up the stair. The door was opened by a youth evidently astounded at the appearance of a client, and I was ushered into the presence of my young friend, who was writing furiously in a large ledger — upside down, as I afterwards discovered.

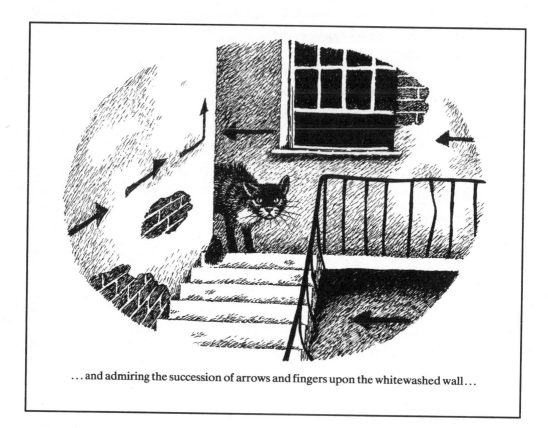

...and admiring the succession of arrows and fingers upon the whitewashed wall...

After the first greetings, I plunged into business at once.

'Look here, Jack,' I said, 'I want you to get me a spirit, if you can.'

'Spirits you mean!' shouted my wife's cousin, plunging his hand into the waste-paper basket and producing a bottle with the celerity of a conjuring trick. 'Let's have a drink!'

I held up my hand as a mute appeal against such a proceeding so early in the day; but on lowering it again I found that I had almost involuntarily closed my fingers round the tumbler which my adviser had pressed upon me. I drank the contents hastily off, lest anyone should come in upon us and set me down as a toper. After all there was something very amusing about the young fellow's eccentricities.

'Not spirits,' I explained smilingly; 'an apparition — a ghost. If such a thing is to be had, I should be very willing to negotiate.'

'A ghost for Goresthorpe Grange?' inquired Mr Brocket, with as much coolness as if I had asked for a drawing-room suite.

'Quite so,' I answered.

'Easiest thing in the world,' said my companion, filling up my glass again in spite of my remonstrance. 'Let us see!' Here he took down a large red notebook, with all the letters of the alphabet in a fringe down the edge. 'A ghost you said, didn't you? That's G. G — gems — gimlets — gas-pipes — gauntlets — guns — galleys. Ah, here we are. Ghosts. Volume nine, section six, page forty-one. Excuse me!' And Jack ran up a ladder and began rummaging among a pile of ledgers on a high shelf. I felt half inclined to empty my glass into the spittoon when his back was turned; but on second thoughts I disposed of it in a legitimate way.

'Here it is!' cried my London agent, jumping off the ladder with a crash, and depositing an enormous volume of manuscript upon the table. 'I have all these things tabulated, so that I may lay my hands upon them in a moment. It's all right — it's quite weak' (here he filled our glasses again). 'What were we looking up, again?'

'Ghosts,' I suggested.

'Of course; page 41. Here we are. "J. H. Fowler & Son, Dunkel Street, suppliers of mediums to the nobility and gentry; charms sold — love-philtres — mummies — horoscopes cast." Nothing in your line there, I suppose?'

I shook my head despondently.

'Frederick Tabb,' continued my wife's cousin, 'sole channel of communication between the living and the dead. Proprietor of the spirits of Byron, Kirke White, Grimaldi, Tom Cribb, and Inigo Jones. That's about the figure!'

'Nothing romantic enough there,' I objected. 'Good heavens! Fancy a ghost with a black eye and a handkerchief tied round its waist, or turning somersaults, and saying, "How are you tomorrow?" The very idea made me so warm that I emptied my glass and filled it again.

'Here is another,' said my companion, '"Christopher McCarthy; bi-weekly séances — attended by all the eminent spirits of ancient and modern times. Nativities — charms — abracadabras, messages from the

dead." He might be able to help us. However, I shall have a hunt round
myself tomorrow, and see some of these fellows. I know their haunts, and
it's odd if I can't pick up something cheap. So there's an end of business,' he
concluded, hurling the ledger into the corner, 'and now we'll have
something to drink.'

We had several things to drink — so many that my inventive faculties
were dulled next morning, and I had some little difficulty in explaining to
Mrs D'Odd why it was that I hung my boots and spectacles upon a peg along
with my other garments before retiring to rest. The new hopes excited by
the confident manner in which my agent had undertaken the commission
caused me to rise superior to alcoholic reaction, and I paced about the
rambling corridors and old-fashioned rooms, picturing to myself the
appearance of my expected acquisition, and deciding what part of the
building would harmonize best with its presence. After much consideration,
I pitched upon the banqueting-hall as being, on the whole, most suitable for
its reception. It was a long low room, hung round with valuable tapestry and
interesting relics of the old family to whom it had belonged. Coats of mail
and implements of war glimmered fitfully as the light of the fire played over
them, and the wind crept under the door, moving the hangings to and fro
with a ghastly rustling. At one end there was the raised dais, on which in
ancient times the host and his guests used to spread their table, while
a descent of a couple of steps led to the lower part of the hall, where the
vassals and retainers held wassail. The floor was uncovered by any sort of
carpet, but a layer of rushes had been scattered over it by my direction. In
the whole room there was nothing to remind one of the nineteenth century;
except, indeed, my own solid silver plate, stamped with the resuscitated
family arms, which was laid out upon an oak table in the centre. This,
I determined, should be the haunted room, supposing my wife's cousin to
succeed in his negotiation with the spirit-mongers. There was nothing for it
now but to wait patiently until I heard some news of the result of his
inquiries.

A letter came in the course of a few days, which, if it was short, was at
least encouraging. It was scribbled in pencil on the back of a playbill, and
sealed apparently with a tobacco-stopper. 'Am on the track,' it said.
'Nothing of the sort to be had from any professional spiritualist, but picked
up a fellow in a pub yesterday who says he can manage it for you. Will send
him down unless you wire to the contrary. Abrahams is his name, and he has
done one or two of these jobs before.' The letter wound up with some

incoherent allusions to a cheque, and was signed by my affectionate cousin, John Brocket.

I need hardly say that I did not wire, but awaited the arrival of Mr Abrahams with all impatience. In spite of my belief in the supernatural, I could scarcely credit the fact that any mortal could have such a command over the spirit-world as to deal in them and barter them against mere earthly gold. Still, I had Jack's word for it that such a trade existed; and here was a gentleman with a Judaical name ready to demonstrate it by proof positive. How vulgar and commonplace Jorrocks' eighteenth-century ghost would appear should I succeed in securing a real mediaeval apparition! I almost thought that one had been sent down in advance, for, as I walked round the moat that night before retiring to rest, I came upon a dark figure engaged in surveying the machinery of my portcullis and drawbridge. His start of surprise, however, and the manner in which he hurried off into the darkness, speedily convinced me of his earthly origin, and I put him down as some admirer of one of my female retainers mourning over the muddy Hellespont which divided him from his love. Whoever he may have been, he disappeared and did not return, though I loitered about for some time in the hope of catching a glimpse of him and exercising my feudal rights upon his person.

Jack Brocket was as good as his word. The shades of another evening were beginning to darken round Goresthorpe Grange, when a peal at the outer bell, and the sound of a fly pulling up, announced the arrival of Mr Abrahams. I hurried down to meet him, half expecting to see a choice assortment of ghosts crowding in at his rear. Instead, however, of being the sallow-faced, melancholy-eyed man that I had pictured to myself, the ghost-dealer was a sturdy little podgy fellow, with a pair of wonderfully keen sparkling eyes and a mouth which was constantly stretched in a good-humoured, if somewhat artificial, grin. His sole stock-in-trade seemed to consist of a small leather bag jealously locked and strapped, which emitted a metallic chink upon being placed on the stone flags of the hall.

'And 'ow are you, sir?' he asked, wringing my hand with the utmost effusion. 'And the missus, 'ow is she? And all the others — 'ow's all their 'ealth?'

I intimated that we were all as well as could reasonably be expected; but Mr Abrahams happened to catch a glimpse of Mrs D'Odd in the distance, and at once plunged at her with another string of inquiries as to her

health, delivered so volubly and with such an intense earnestness that I half
expected to see him terminate his cross-examination by feeling her pulse
and demanding a sight of her tongue. All this time his little eyes rolled
round and round, shifting perpetually from the floor to the ceiling, and from
the ceiling to the walls, taking in apparently every article of furniture in
a single comprehensive glance.

Having satisfied himself that neither of us was in a pathological
condition, Mr Abrahams suffered me to lead him upstairs, where a repast
had been laid out for him to which he did ample justice. The mysterious
little bag he carried along with him, and deposited it under his chair during
the meal. It was not until the table had been cleared and we were left
together that he broached the matter on which he had come down.

'I hunderstand,' he remarked, puffing at a trichinopoly, 'that you want
my 'elp in fitting up this 'ere 'ouse with a happarition.'

I acknowledged the correctness of his surmise, while mentally
wondering at those restless eyes of his, which still danced about the room as
if he were making an inventory of the contents.

'And you won't find a better man for the job, though I says it as
shouldn't,' continued my companion. 'Wot did I say to the young gent wot
spoke to me in the bar of the Lame Dog? "Can you do it?" says he. "Try
me," says I, "me and my bag. Just try me." I couldn't say fairer than that.'

My respect for Jack Brocket's business capacities began to go up very
considerably. He certainly seemed to have managed the matter wonderfully
well. 'You don't mean to say that you carry ghosts about in bags!'
I remarked, with diffidence.

Mr Abrahams smiled a smile of superior knowledge. 'You wait,' he
said; 'give me the right place and the right hour, with a little of the essence of
Lucoptolycus' — here he produced a small bottle from his waistcoat-pocket
— 'and you won't find no ghost that I ain't up to. You'll see them yourself,
and pick your own, and I can't say fairer than that.'

As all Mr Abrahams' protestations of fairness were accompanied by
a cunning leer and a wink from one or other of his wicked little eyes, the
impression of candour was somewhat weakened.

'When are you going to do it?' I asked reverentially.

'Ten minutes to one in the morning,' said Mr Abrahams, with decision.
'Some says midnight, but I says ten to one, when there ain't such a crowd,
and you can pick your own ghost. And now,' he continued, rising to his feet,
'suppose you trot me round the premises, and let me see where you wants it;

A.C.Doyle

for there's some places as attracts 'em, and some as they won't hear of — not if there was no other place in the world.'

Mr Abrahams inspected our corridors and chambers with a most critical and observant eye, fingering the old tapestry with the air of a connoisseur, and remarking in an undertone that it would 'match uncommon nice.' It was not until he reached the banqueting-hall, however, which I had myself picked out, that his admiration reached the pitch of enthusiasm. ''Ere's the place!' he shouted, dancing, bag in hand, round the table on which my plate was lying, and looking not unlike some quaint little goblin himself. ' 'Ere's the place; we won't get nothin' to beat this! A fine room — noble, solid, none of your electroplate trash! That's the way as things ought to be done, sir. Plenty of room for 'em to glide here. Send up some brandy and the box of weeds; I'll sit here by the fire and do the preliminaries, which is more trouble than you'd think; for them ghosts carries on hawful at times, before they finds out who they've got to deal with. If you was in the room they'd tear you to pieces as like as not. You leave me alone to tackle them, and at half-past twelve come in, and I lay they'll be quiet enough by then.'

Mr Abrahams' request struck me as a reasonable one, so I left him with his feet upon the mantel-piece, and his chair in front of the fire, fortifying himself with stimulants against his refractory visitors. From the room beneath, in which I sat with Mrs D'Odd, I could hear that after sitting for some time he rose up, and paced about the hall with quick impatient steps. We then heard him try the lock of the door, and afterwards drag some heavy article of furniture in the direction of the window, on which, apparently, he mounted, for I heard the creaking of the rusty hinges as the diamond-paned casement folded backwards, and I knew it to be situated several feet above the little man's reach. Mrs D'Odd says that she could distinguish his voice speaking in low and rapid whispers after this, but that may have been her imagination. I confess that I began to feel more impressed than I had deemed it possible to be. There was something awesome in the thought of the solitary mortal standing by the open window and summoning in from the gloom outside the spirits of the nether world. It was with a trepidation which I could hardly disguise from Matilda that I observed that the clock was pointing to half-past twelve, and that the time had come for me to share the vigil of my visitor.

He was sitting in his old position when I entered, and there were no signs of the mysterious movements which I had overheard, though his chubby face was flushed as with recent exertion.

'Are you succeeding all right?' I asked as I came in, putting on as careless an air as possible, but glancing involuntarily round the room to see if we were alone.

'Only your help is needed to complete the matter,' said Mr Abrahams, in a solemn voice. 'You shall sit by me and partake of the essence of Lucoptolycus, which removes the scales from our earthly eyes. Whatever you may chance to see, speak not and make no movement, lest you break the spell.' His manner was subdued, and his usual cockney vulgarity had entirely disappeared. I took the chair which he indicated, and awaited the result.

My companion cleared the rushes from the floor in our neighbour-hood, and, going down upon his hands and knees, described a half-circle with chalk, which enclosed the fireplace and ourselves. Round the edge of this half-circle he drew several hieroglyphics, not unlike the signs of the zodiac. He then stood up and uttered a long invocation, delivered so rapidly that it sounded like a single gigantic word in some uncouth guttural language. Having finished this prayer, if prayer it was, he pulled out the small bottle which he had produced before, and poured a couple of teaspoonfuls of clear transparent fluid into a phial, which he handed to me with an intimation that I should drink it.

The liquid had a faintly sweet odour, not unlike the aroma of certain sorts of apples. I hesitated a moment before applying it to my lips, but an impatient gesture from my companion overcame my scruples, and I tossed it off. The taste was not unpleasant; and, as it gave rise to no immediate effects, I leaned back in my chair and composed myself for what was to come. Mr Abrahams seated himself beside me, and I felt that he was watching my face from time to time while repeating some more of the invocations in which he had indulged before.

A sense of delicious warmth and languor began gradually to steal over me, partly, perhaps, from the heat of the fire, and partly from some unexplained cause. An uncontrollable impulse to sleep weighed down my eyelids, while, at the same time, my brain worked actively, and a hundred beautiful and pleasing ideas flitted through it. So utterly lethargic did I feel that, though I was aware that my companion put his hand over the region of my heart, as if to feel how it were beating, I did not attempt to prevent him, nor did I even ask him for the reason of his action. Everything in the room appeared to be reeling slowly round in a drowsy dance, of which I was the centre. The great elk's head at the far end wagged solemnly backwards and forwards, while the massive salvers on the tables performed cotillons with the claret-cooler and the epergne. My head fell upon my breast from sheer heaviness, and I should have become unconscious had I not been recalled to myself by the opening of the door at the other end of the hall.

This door led on to the raised dais, which, as I have mentioned, the heads of the house used to reserve for their own use. As it swung slowly back upon its hinges, I sat up in my chair, clutching at the arms, and staring

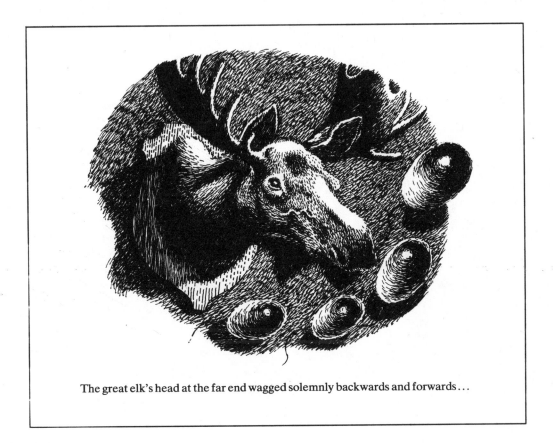

The great elk's head at the far end wagged solemnly backwards and forwards...

with a horrified glare at the dark passage outside. Something was coming down it — something unformed and intangible, but still a *something*. Dim and shadowy, I saw it flit across the threshold, while a blast of ice-cold air swept down the room, which seemed to blow through me, chilling my very heart. I was aware of the mysterious presence, and then I heard it speak in a voice like the sighing of an east wind among pine-trees on the banks of a desolate sea.

It said: 'I am the invisible nonentity. I have affinities and am subtle.

I am electric, magnetic, and spiritualistic. I am the great ethereal sigh-heaver. I kill dogs. Mortal, wilt thou choose me?'

I was about to speak, but the words seemed to be choked in my throat; and, before I could get them out, the shadow flitted across the hall and vanished in the darkness at the other side, while a long-drawn melancholy sigh quivered through the apartment.

I turned my eyes towards the door once more, and beheld, to my

I am the great ethereal sigh-heaver. I kill dogs.

astonishment, a very small old woman, who hobbled along the corridor and into the hall. She passed backwards and forwards several times, and then, crouching down at the very edge of the circle upon the floor, she disclosed a face the horrible malignity of which shall never be banished from my recollection. Every foul passion appeared to have left its mark upon that hideous countenance.

'Ha! ha!' she screamed, holding out her wizened hands like the talons of an unclean bird. 'You see what I am. I am the fiendish old woman. I wear snuff-coloured silks. My curse descends on people. Sir Walter was partial to me. Shall I be thine, mortal?'

I endeavoured to shake my head in horror; on which she aimed a blow at me with her crutch, and vanished with an eldritch scream.

By this time my eyes turned naturally towards the open door, and I was hardly surprised to see a man walk in of tall and noble stature. His face was deadly pale, but was surmounted by a fringe of dark hair which fell in ringlets down his back. A short pointed beard covered his chin. He was dressed in loose-fitting clothes, made apparently of yellow satin, and a large white ruff surrounded his neck. He paced across the room with slow and majestic strides. Then turning, he addressed me in a sweet, exquisitely-modulated voice.

'I am the cavalier,' he remarked. 'I pierce and am pierced. Here is my rapier. I clink steel. This is a blood-stain over my heart. I can emit hollow groans. I am patronized by many old conservative families. I am the original manor-house apparition. I work alone, or in company with shrieking damsels.'

He bent his head courteously, as though awaiting my reply, but the same choking sensation prevented me from speaking; and, with a deep bow, he disappeared.

He had hardly gone before a feeling of intense horror stole over me, and I was aware of the presence of a ghastly creature in the room of dim outlines and uncertain proportions. One moment it seemed to pervade the entire apartment, while at another it would become invisible, but always leaving behind it a distinct consciousness of its presence. Its voice, when it spoke, was quavering and gusty. It said, 'I am the leaver of footsteps and the spiller of gouts of blood. I tramp upon corridors. Charles Dickens has alluded to me. I make strange and disagreeable noises. I snatch letters and place invisible hands on people's wrists. I am cheerful. I burst into peals of hideous laughter. Shall I do one now?' I raised my hand in a deprecating way, but too late to prevent one discordant outbreak which echoed through the room. Before I could lower it the apparition was gone.

I turned my head towards the door in time to see a man come hastily and stealthily into the chamber. He was a sunburnt powerfully-built fellow, with earrings in his ears and a Barcelona handkerchief tied loosely round his neck. His head was bent upon his chest, and his whole aspect was that of one afflicted by intolerable remorse. He paced rapidly backwards and forwards like a caged tiger, and I observed that a drawn knife glittered in one of his hands, while he grasped what appeared to be a piece of parchment in the other. His voice, when he spoke, was deep and sonorous. He said, 'I am a murderer. I am a ruffian. I crouch when I walk. I step noiselessly. I know something of the Spanish Main. I can do the lost treasure business. I have charts. Am able-bodied and a good walker. Capable of haunting a large park.' He looked towards me beseechingly, but before I could make a sign I was paralysed by the horrible sight which appeared at the door.

It was a very tall man, if, indeed, it might be called a man, for the gaunt bones were protruding through the corroding flesh, and the features were of a leaden hue. A winding-sheet was wrapped round the figure, and formed a hood over the head, from under the shadow of which two fiendish eyes, deep-set in their grisly sockets, blazed and sparkled like red-hot coals. The lower jaw had fallen upon the breast, disclosing a withered, shrivelled tongue and two lines of black and jagged fangs. I shuddered and drew back as this fearful apparition advanced to the edge of the circle.

'I am the American blood-curdler,' it said, in a voice which seemed to come in a hollow murmur from the earth beneath it. 'None other is genuine. I am the embodiment of Edgar Allan Poe. I am circumstantial and horrible. I am a low-caste spirit-subduing spectre. Observe my blood and my bones. I am grisly and nauseous. No depending on artificial aid. Work with grave-clothes, a coffin-lid, and a galvanic battery. Turn hair white in a night.' The creature stretched out its fleshless arms to me as if in entreaty, but I shook my head; and it vanished, leaving a low, sickening, repulsive odour behind it. I sank back in my chair, so overcome by terror and disgust that I would have very willingly resigned myself to dispensing with a ghost altogether, could I have been sure that this was the last of the hideous procession.

A faint sound of trailing garments warned me that it was not so. I looked up, and beheld a white figure emerging from the corridor into the light. As it stepped across the threshold I saw that it was that of a young and beautiful woman dressed in the fashion of a bygone day. Her hands were clasped in front of her, and her pale proud face bore traces of passion and of suffering. She crossed the hall with a gentle sound, like the rustling of autumn leaves, and then, turning her lovely and unutterably sad eyes upon me, she said,

'I am the plaintive and sentimental, the beautiful and ill-used. I have

A. C. Doyle

been forsaken and betrayed. I shriek in the night-time and glide down passages. My antecedents are highly respectable and generally aristocratic. My tastes are aesthetic. Old oak furniture like this would do, with a few more coats of mail and plenty of tapestry. Will you not take me?'

Her voice died away in beautiful cadence as she concluded, and she held out her hands as if in supplication. I am always sensitive to female influences. Besides, what would Jorrocks' ghost be to this? Could anything be in better taste? Would I not be exposing myself to the chance of injuring my nervous system by interviews with such creatures as my last visitor, unless I decided at once? She gave me a seraphic smile, as if she knew what was passing in my mind. That smile settled the matter. 'She will do!' I cried; 'I choose this one;' and as, in my enthusiasm, I took a step towards her I passed over the magic circle which had girdled me round.

'Argentine, we have been robbed!'

I had an indistinct consciousness of these words being spoken, or rather screamed, in my ear a great number of times without my being able to grasp their meaning. A violent throbbing in my head seemed to adapt itself to their rhythm, and I closed my eyes to the lullaby of 'Robbed, robbed, robbed.' A vigorous shake caused me to open them again, however, and the sight of Mrs D'Odd in the scantiest of costumes and most furious of tempers was sufficiently impressive to recall all my scattered thoughts, and make me realize that I was lying on my back on the floor, with my head among the ashes which had fallen from last night's fire, and a small glass phial in my hand.

I staggered to my feet, but felt so weak and giddy that I was compelled to fall back into a chair. As my brain became clearer, stimulated by the exclamations of Matilda, I began gradually to recollect the events of the night. There was the door through which my supernatural visitors had filed. There was the circle of chalk with the hieroglyphics round the edge. There was the cigar-box and brandy-bottle which had been honoured by the attentions of Mr Abrahams. But the seer himself — where was he? and what was this open window with a rope running out of it? And where, O where, was the pride of Goresthorpe Grange, the glorious plate which was to have been the delectation of generations of D'Odds? And why was Mrs D. standing in the grey light of dawn, wringing her hands and repeating her monotonous refrain? It was only very gradually that my misty brain took these things in, and grasped the connection between them.

Reader, I have never seen Mr Abrahams since; I have never seen the plate stamped with the resuscitated family crest; hardest of all, I have never caught a glimpse of the melancholy spectre with the trailing garments, nor do I expect that I ever shall. In fact my night's experiences have cured me of my mania for the supernatural, and quite reconciled me to inhabiting the humdrum nineteenth-century edifice on the outskirts of London which Mrs D. has long had in her mind's eye.

As to the explanation of all that occurred — that is a matter which is

...and what was this open window with a rope running out of it?

open to several surmises. That Mr Abrahams, the ghost-hunter, was identical with Jemmy Wilson, *alias* the Nottingham crackster, is considered more than probable at Scotland Yard, and certainly the description of that remarkable burglar tallied very well with the appearance of my visitor. The small bag which I have described was picked up in a neighbouring field next day, and found to contain a choice assortment of jemmies and centrebits.

Footmarks deeply imprinted in the mud on either side of the moat showed that an accomplice from below had received the sack of precious metals which had been let down through the open window. No doubt the pair of scoundrels, while looking round for a job, had overheard Jack Brocket's indiscreet inquiries, and had promptly availed themselves of the tempting opening.

And now as to my less substantial visitors, and the curious grotesque vision which I had enjoyed — am I to lay it down to any real power over occult matters possessed by my Nottingham friend? For a long time I was doubtful upon the point, and eventually endeavoured to solve it by consulting a well-known analyst and medical man, sending him the few drops of the so-called essence of Lucoptolycus which remained in my phial. I append the letter which I received from him, only too happy to have the opportunity of winding up my little narrative by the weighty words of a man of learning.

'*Arundel Street.*

'DEAR SIR, — Your very singular case has interested me extremely. The bottle which you sent contained a strong solution of chloral, and the quantity which you describe yourself as having swallowed must have amounted to at least eighty grains of the pure hydrate. This would of course have reduced you to a partial state of insensibility, gradually going on to complete coma. In this semi-unconscious state of chloralism it is not unusual for circumstantial and *bizarre* visions to present themselves — more especially to individuals unaccustomed to the use of the drug. You tell me in your note that your mind was saturated with ghostly literature, and that you had long taken a morbid interest in classifying and recalling the various forms in which apparitions have been said to appear. You must also remember that you were expecting to see something of that very nature, and that your nervous system was worked up to an unnatural state of tension. Under the circumstances, I think that, far from the sequel being an astonishing one, it would have been very surprising indeed to anyone versed in narcotics had you not experienced some such effects. — I remain, dear sir, sincerely yours,

'T. E. STUBE, M. D.

'Argentine D'Odd, Esq.
    'The Elms, Brixton.'

Charles Dickens
THE SIGNALMAN

'Halloa! Below there!'

When he heard a voice thus calling to him, he was standing at the door of his box, with a flag in his hand, furled round its short pole. One would have thought, considering the nature of the ground, that he could not have doubted from what quarter the voice came; but, instead of looking up to where I stood on the top of the steep cutting nearly over his head, he turned himself about and looked down the Line. There was something remarkable

'Halloa! Below!' From looking down the Line, he turned himself about again, and, raising his eyes, saw my figure high above him.

in his manner of doing so, though I could not have said for my life, what. But, I know it was remarkable enough to attract my notice, even though his figure was foreshortened and shadowed, down in the deep trench, and mine was high above him, so steeped in the glow of an angry sunset that I had shaded my eyes with my hand before I saw him at all.

'Halloa! Below!'

From looking down the Line, he turned himself about again, and, raising his eyes, saw my figure high above him.

'Is there any path by which I can come down and speak to you?'

He looked up at me without replying, and I looked down at him without pressing him too soon with a repetition of my idle question. Just then, there came a vague vibration in the earth and air, quickly changing into a violent pulsation, and an oncoming rush that caused me to start back, as though it had force to draw me down. When such vapour as rose to my height from this rapid train, had passed me and was skimming away over the landscape, I looked down again, and saw him re-furling the flag he had shown while the train went by.

I repeated my inquiry. After a pause, during which he seemed to regard me with fixed attention, he motioned with his rolled-up flag towards a point on my level, some two or three hundred yards distant, I called down to him, 'All right!' and made for that point. There, by dint of looking closely about me, I found a rough zig-zag descending path notched out: which I followed.

The cutting was extremely deep, and unusually precipitate. It was made through a clammy stone that became oozier and wetter as I went down. For these reasons, I found the way long enough to give me time to recall a singular air of reluctance or compulsion with which he had pointed out the path.

When I came down low enough upon the zig-zag descent, to see him again, I saw that he was standing between the rails on the way by which the train had lately passed, in an attitude as if he were waiting for me to appear. He had his left hand at his chin, and that left elbow rested on his right hand crossed over his breast. His attitude was one of such expectation and watchfulness, that I stopped a moment, wondering at it.

I resumed my downward way, and, stepping out upon the level of the railroad and drawing nearer to him, saw that he was a dark sallow man, with a dark beard and rather heavy eyebrows. His post was in as solitary and dismal a place as ever I saw. On either side, a dripping-wet wall of jagged stone, excluding all view but a strip of sky; the perspective one way, only a crooked prolongation of this great dungeon; the shorter perspective in the other direction, terminating in a gloomy red light, and the gloomier entrance to a black tunnel, in whose massive architecture there was a barbarous, depressing, and forbidding air. So little sunlight ever found its way to this spot, that it had an earthy deadly smell; and so much cold wind rushed through it, that it struck chill to me, as if I had left the natural world.

Before he stirred, I was near enough to him to have touched him. Not even then removing his eyes from mine, he stepped back one step, and lifted his hand.

This was a lonesome post to occupy (I said), and it had riveted my attention when I looked down from up yonder. A visitor was a rarity, I should suppose; not an unwelcome rarity, I hoped? In me, he merely saw a man who had been shut up within narrow limits all his life, and who, being at last set free, had a newly-awakened interest in these great works. To such purpose I spoke to him; but I am far from sure of the terms I used, for, besides that I am not happy in opening any conversation, there was something in the man that daunted me.

He directed a most curious look towards the red light near the tunnel's mouth, and looked all about it, as if something were missing from it, and then looked at me.

That light was part of his charge? Was it not?

He answered in a low voice: 'Don't you know it is?'

The monstrous thought came into my mind as I perused the fixed eyes and the saturnine face, that this was a spirit, not a man. I have speculated since, whether there may have been infection in his mind.

In my turn, I stepped back. But in making the action, I detected in his eyes some latent fear of me. This put the monstrous thought to flight.

'You look at me,' I said, forcing a smile, 'as if you had a dread of me.'

'I was doubtful,' he returned, 'whether I had seen you before.'

'Where?'

He pointed to the red light he had looked at.

'There?' I said.

Intently watchful of me, he replied (but without sound), Yes.

'My good fellow, what should I do there? However, be that as it may, I never was there, you may swear.'

'I think I may,' he rejoined. 'Yes. I am sure I may.'

His manner cleared, like my own. He replied to my remarks with readiness, and in well-chosen words. Had he much to do there? Yes; that was to say, he had enough responsibility to bear; but exactness and watchfulness were what was required of him, and of actual work — manual labour — he had next to none. To change that signal, to trim those lights, and to turn this iron handle now and then, was all he had to do under that head. Regarding those many long and lonely hours of which I seemed to make so much, he could only say that the routine of his life had shaped itself into that form, and he had grown used to it. He had taught himself a language down here – if only to know it by sight, and to have formed his own crude ideas of its pronunciation, could be called learning it. He had also worked at fractions and decimals, and tried a little algebra; but he was, and had been as a boy, a poor hand at figures. Was it necessary for him when on duty, always to remain in that channel of damp air, and could he never rise into the sunshine from between those high stone walls? Why, that depended upon times and circumstances. Under some conditions there would be less upon the Line than under others, and the same held good as to certain hours of the day and night. In bright weather, he did choose occasions for getting a little above these lower shadows; but, being at all times liable to be called by his electric bell, and at such times listening for it with redoubled anxiety, the relief was less than I would suppose.

He took me into his box, where there was a fire, a desk for an official book in which he had to make certain entries, a telegraphic instrument with its dial face and needles, and the little bell of which he had spoken. On my trusting that he would excuse the remark that he had been well educated, and (I hoped I might say without offence), perhaps educated above that station, he observed that instances of slight incongruity in such-wise would rarely be found wanting among large bodies of men; that he had heard it was so in workhouses, in the police force, even in that last desperate resource, the army; and that he knew it was so, more or less, in any great railway staff. He had been, when young (if I could believe it, sitting in that hut; he scarcely could), a student of natural philosophy, and had attended lectures; but he had run wild, misused his opportunities, gone down, and never risen again. He had no complaint to offer about that. He had made his bed, and he lay upon it. It was far too late to make another.

'All that I have here condensed,' he said in a quiet manner, with his grave dark regards divided between me and the fire. He threw in the word 'Sir', from time to time, and especially when he referred to his youth: as though to request me to understand that he claimed to be nothing but what I found him.

He was several times interrupted by the little bell, and had to read off messages, and send replies. Once, he had to stand without the door, and display a flag as a train passed, and make some verbal communication to the driver. In the discharge of his duties I observed him to be remarkably exact and vigilant, breaking off his discourse at a syllable, and remaining silent until what he had to do was done.

In a word, I should have set this man down as one of the safest of men to be employed in that capacity, but for the circumstance that while he was speaking to me he twice broke off with a fallen colour, turned his face towards the little bell when it did NOT ring, opened the door of the hut (which was kept shut to exclude the unhealthy damp), and looked out towards the red light near the mouth of the tunnel. On both of those occasions, he came back to the fire with the inexplicable air upon him which I had remarked, without being able to define, when we were so far asunder.

Said I when I rose to leave him: 'You almost make me think that I have met with a contented man.'

(I am afraid I must acknowledge that I said it to lead him on.)

'I believe I used to be so,' he rejoined, in the low voice in which he had first spoken; 'but I am troubled, sir, I am troubled.'

He would have recalled the words if he could. He had said them, however, and I took them up quickly.

'With what? What is your trouble?'

'It is very difficult to impart, sir. It is very, very difficult to speak of. If ever you make me another visit, I will try to tell you.'

'But I expressly intend to make you another visit. Say, when shall it be?'

'I go off early in the morning, and I shall be on again at ten tomorrow night, sir.'

'I will come at eleven.'

He thanked me, and went out at the door with me. 'I'll show my white light, sir,' he said, in his peculiar low voice, 'till you have found the way up. When you have found it, don't call out! And when you are at the top, don't call out!'

His manner seemed to make the place strike colder to me, but I said no more than 'Very well.'

'And when you come down tomorrow night, don't call out! Let me ask you a parting question. What made you cry "Halloa! Below there!" tonight?'

'Heaven knows,' said I. 'I cried something to that effect —'

'Not to that effect, sir. Those were the very words. I know them well.'

'Admit those were the very words. I said them, no doubt, because I saw you below.'

'For no other reason?'

'What other reason could I possibly have?'

'You have no feeling that they were conveyed to you in any supernatural way?'

'No.'

He wished me good night, and held up his light. I walked by the side of the down Line of rails (with a very disagreeable sensation of a train coming behind me), until I found the path. It was easier to mount than to descend, and I got back to my inn without any adventure.

Punctual to my appointment, I placed my foot on the first notch of the zig-zag next night, as the distant clocks were striking eleven. He was waiting for me at the bottom, with his white light on. 'I have not called out,' I said, when we came close together; 'may I speak now?' 'By all means, sir.' 'Good night then, and here's my hand.' 'Good night, sir, and here's mine.' With that, we walked side by side to his box, entered it, closed the door, and sat down by the fire.

'I have made up my mind, sir,' he began, bending forward as soon as we were seated, and speaking in a tone but a little above a whisper, 'that you shall not have to ask me twice what troubles me. I took you for someone else yesterday evening. That troubles me.'

'That mistake?'

'No. That someone else.'

'Who is it?'

'I don't know.'

'Like me?'

'I don't know. I never saw the face. The left arm is across the face, and the right arm is waved. Violently waved. This way.'

I followed his action with my eyes, and it was the action of an arm gesticulating with the utmost passion and vehemence: 'For God's sake clear the way!'

'One moonlight night,' said the man, 'I was sitting here, when I heard a voice cry "Halloa! Below there!" I started up, looked from that door, and saw this Someone else standing by the red light near the tunnel, waving as I just now showed you. The voice seemed hoarse with shouting, and it cried, "Look out! Look out!" And then again "Halloa! Below there! Look out!" I caught up my lamp, turned it on red, and ran towards the figure, calling,

"What's wrong? What has happened? Where?" It stood just outside the blackness of the tunnel. I advanced so close upon it that I wondered at its keeping the sleeve across its eyes. I ran right up at it, and had my hand stretched out to pull the sleeve away, when it was gone.'

'Into the tunnel,' said I.

'No. I ran on into the tunnel, five hundred yards. I stopped and held my lamp above my head, and saw the figures of the measured distance, and saw

The left arm is across the face, and the right arm is waved. Violently waved.

the wet stains stealing down the walls and trickling through the arch. I ran out again, faster than I had run in (for I had a mortal abhorrence of the place upon me), and I looked all round the red light with my own red light, and I went up the iron ladder to the gallery atop of it, and I came down again, and ran back here. I telegraphed both ways: "An alarm has been given. Is anything wrong?" The answer came back, both ways: "All well."

Resisting the slow touch of a frozen finger tracing out my spine, I showed him how that this figure must be a deception of his sense of sight, and how that figures, originating in disease of the delicate nerves that minister to the functions of the eye, were known to have often troubled patients, some of whom had become conscious of the nature of their affliction, and had even proved it by experiments upon themselves. 'As to an imaginary cry,' said I, 'do but listen for a moment to the wind in this unnatural valley while we speak so low, and to the wild harp it makes of the telegraph wires!'

That was all very well, he returned, after we had sat listening for a while, and he ought to know something of the wind and the wires, he who so often passed long winter nights there, alone and watching. But he would beg to remark that he had not finished.

I asked his pardon, and he slowly added these words, touching my arm!

'Within six hours after the Appearance, the memorable accident on this Line happened, and within ten hours the dead and wounded were brought along through the tunnel over the spot where the figure had stood.'

A disagreeable shudder crept over me, but I did my best against it. It was not to be denied, I rejoined, that this was a remarkable coincidence, calculated deeply to impress his mind. But, it was unquestionable that remarkable coincidences did continually occur, and they must be taken into account in dealing with such a subject. Though to be sure I must admit, I added (for I thought I saw that he was going to bring the objection to bear upon me), men of common sense did not allow much for coincidences in making the ordinary calculations of life.

He again begged to remark that he had not finished.

I again begged his pardon for being betrayed into interruptions.

'This,' he said, again laying his hand upon my arm, and glancing over his shoulder with hollow eyes, 'was just a year ago. Six or seven months passed, and I had recovered from the surprise and shock, when one morning, as the day was breaking, I, standing at that door, looked towards the red light, and saw the spectre again.' He stopped, with a fixed look at me.

'Did it cry out?'

'No. It was silent.'

'Did it wave its arm?'

Charles Dickens

'No. It leaned against the shaft of the light, with both hands before the face. Like this.'

Once more, I followed his action with my eyes. It was an action of mourning. I have seen such an attitude in stone figures on tombs.

'Did you go up to it?'

'I came in and sat down, partly to collect my thoughts, partly because it had turned me faint. When I went to the door again, daylight was above me, and the ghost was gone.'

A beautiful young lady...was brought in here, and laid down on this floor...

'But nothing followed? Nothing came of this?'

He touched me on the arm with his forefinger twice or thrice, giving a ghastly nod each time:

'That very day, as a train came out of the tunnel, I noticed, at a carriage window on my side, what looked like a confusion of hands and heads, and something waved. I saw it, just in time to signal the driver, Stop! He shut off, and put his brake on, but the train drifted past here a hundred and fifty yards or more. I ran after it, and, as I went along, heard terrible screams and cries. A beautiful young lady had died instantaneously in one of the compartments, and was brought in here, and laid down on this floor between us.'

Involuntarily, I pushed my chair back, as I looked from the boards at which he pointed, to himself.

'True, sir. True. Precisely as it happened, so I tell it you.'

I could think of nothing to say, to any purpose, and my mouth was very dry. The wind and the wires took up the story with a long lamenting wail.

He resumed. 'Now, sir, mark this, and judge how my mind is troubled. The spectre came back, a week ago. Ever since, it has been there, now and again, by fits and starts.'

'At the light?'

'At the Danger-light.'

'What does it seem to do?'

He repeated, if possible with increased passion and vehemence, that former gesticulation of 'For God's sake clear the way!'

Then, he went on. 'I have no peace or rest for it. It calls to me, for many minutes together, in an agonized manner, "Below there! Look out! Look out!" It stands waving to me. It rings my little bell —'

I caught at that. 'Did it ring your bell yesterday evening when I was here, and you went to the door?'

'Twice.'

'Why, see,' said I, 'how your imagination misleads you. My eyes were on the bell, and my ears were open to the bell, and if I am a living man, it did NOT ring at those times. No, nor at any other time, except when it was rung in the natural course of physical things by the station communicating with you.'

He shook his head. 'I have never made a mistake as to that, yet, sir. I have never confused the spectre's ring with the man's. The ghost's ring is a strange vibration in the bell that it derives from nothing else, and I have not asserted that the bell stirs to the eye. I don't wonder that you failed to hear it. But *I* heard it.'

'And did the spectre seem to be there, when you looked out?'

'It WAS there.'

'Both times?'

He repeated firmly: 'Both times.'

'Will you come to the door with me, and look for it now?'

He bit his under-lip as though he were somewhat unwilling, but arose. I opened the door, and stood on the step, while he stood in the doorway. There, was the Danger-light. There, was the dismal mouth of the tunnel. There, were the high wet stone walls of the cutting. There, were the stars above them.

'Do you see it?' I asked him, taking particular note of his face. His eyes were prominent and strained; but not very much more so, perhaps, than my own had been when I had directed them earnestly towards the same spot.

'No,' he answered. 'It is not there.'

'Agreed,' said I.

We went in again, shut the door, and resumed our seats. I was thinking how best to improve this advantage, if it might be called one, when he took up the conversation in such a matter of course way, so assuming that there could be no serious question of fact between us, that I felt myself in the weakest of positions.

'By this time you will fully understand, sir,' he said, 'that what troubles me so dreadfully, is the question, what does the spectre mean?'

I was not sure, I told him, that I did fully understand.

'What is its warning against?' he said, ruminating, with his eyes on the fire, and only by times turning them on me. 'What is the danger? Where is the danger? There is danger overhanging, somewhere on the Line. Some dreadful calamity will happen. It is not to be doubted this third time, after what has gone before. But surely this is a cruel haunting of *me*. What can *I* do!'

He pulled out his handkerchief, and wiped the drops from his heated forehead.

'If I telegraph Danger, on either side of me, or on both, I can give no reason for it,' he went on, wiping the palms of his hands. 'I should get into trouble, and do no good. They would think I was mad. This is the way it would work: Message: "Danger! Take care!" Answer: "What Danger? Where?" Message: "Don't know. But for God's sake take care!" They would displace me. What else could they do?'

His pain of mind was most pitiable to see. It was the mental torture of a conscientious man, oppressed beyond endurance by an unintelligible responsibility involving life.

'When it first stood under the Danger-light,' he went on, putting his dark hair back from his head, and drawing his hands outward across and across his temples in an extremity of feverish distress, 'why not tell me where that accident was to happen — if it must happen? Why not tell me how it could be averted — if it could have been averted? When on its second coming it hid its face, why not tell me instead: "She is going to die. Let them keep her at home?" If it came, on those two occasions, only to show me that its warnings were true, and so to prepare me for the third, why not warn me plainly now? And I, Lord help me! A mere poor signalman on this solitary station! Why not go to somebody with credit to be believed, and power to act!'

When I saw him in this state, I saw that for the poor man's sake, as well as for the public safety, what I had to do for the time was, to compose his mind. Therefore, setting aside all question of reality or unreality between us, I represented to him that whoever thoroughly discharged his duty, must do well, and that at least it was his comfort that he understood his duty, thought he did not understand these confounding Appearances. In this effort I succeeded far better than in the attempt to reason him out of his conviction. He became calm; the occupations incidental to his post as the night advanced, began to make larger demands on his attention; and I left him at two in the morning. I had offered to stay through the night, but he would not hear of it.

That I more than once looked back at the red light as I ascended the pathway, that I did not like the red light, and that I should have slept but poorly if my bed had been under it, I see no reason to conceal. Nor, did I like the two sequences of the accident and the dead girl. I see no reason to conceal that, either.

But, what ran most in my thoughts was the consideration how ought I to act, having become the recipient of this disclosure? I had proved the man to be intelligent, vigilant, painstaking, and exact; but how long might he remain so, in his state of mind? Though in a subordinate position, still he held a most important trust, and would I (for instance) like to stake my own life on the chances of his continuing to execute it with precision?

Unable to overcome a feeling that there would be something treacherous in my communicating what he had told me, to his superiors in the Company, without first being plain with himself and proposing a middle course to him, I ultimately resolved to offer to accompany him (otherwise keeping his secret for the present) to the wisest medical practitioner we could hear of in those parts, and to take his opinion. A change in his time of duty would come round next night, he had apprised me, and he would be off an hour or two after sunrise, and on again soon after sunset. I had appointed to return accordingly.

Next evening was a lovely evening, and I walked out early to enjoy it. The sun was not yet quite down when I traversed the fieldpath near the top of the deep cutting. I would extend my walk for an hour, I said to myself, half an hour on and half an hour back, and it would then be time to go to my signalman's box.

The sun was not yet quite down when I traversed the fieldpath...

Before pursuing my stroll, I stepped to the brink, and mechanically looked down, from the point from which I had first seen him. I cannot describe the thrill that seized upon me, when, close at the mouth of the tunnel, I saw the appearance of a man, with his left sleeve across his eyes, passionately waving his right arm.

The nameless horror that oppressed me, passed in a moment, for in a moment I saw that this appearance of a man was a man indeed, and that there was a little group of other men standing at a short distance, to whom he seemed to be rehearsing the gesture he made. The Danger-light was not yet lighted. Against its shaft, a little low hut, entirely new to me, had been made of some wooden supports and tarpaulin. It looked no bigger than a bed.

With an irresistible sense that something was wrong — with a flashing self-reproachful fear that fatal mischief had come of my leaving the man there, and causing no one to be sent to overlook or correct what he did — I descended the notched path with all the speed I could make.

'What is the matter?' I asked the men.

'Signalman killed this morning, sir.'

'Not the man belonging to that box?'

'Yes, sir.'

'Not the man I know?'

'You will recognize him, sir, if you knew him,' said the man who spoke for the others, solemnly uncovering his own head and raising an end of the tarpaulin, 'for his face is quite composed.'

'O! How did this happen, how did this happen?' I asked, turning from one to another as the hut closed in again.

'He was cut down by an engine, sir. No man in England knew his work better. But somehow he was not clear of the outer rail. It was just at broad day. He had struck the light, and had the lamp in his hand. As the engine came out of the tunnel, his back was towards her, and she cut him down. That man drove her, and was showing how it happened. Show the gentleman, Tom.'

The man, who wore a rough dark dress, stepped back to his former place at the mouth of the tunnel:

'Coming round the curve in the tunnel, sir,' he said, 'I saw him at the end, like as if I saw him down a perspective-glass. There was no time to check speed, and I knew him to be very careful. As he didn't seem to take heed of the whistle, I shut it off when we were running down upon him, and called to him as loud as I could call.'

'What did you say?'

'I said, "Below there! Look out! Look out! For God's sake clear the way!"'

I started.

'Ah! It was a dreadful time, sir. I never left off calling to him. I put this arm before my eyes, not to see, and I waved this arm to the last; but it was no use.'

Without prolonging the narrative to dwell on any one of its curious circumstances more than on any other, I may, in closing it, point out the coincidence that the warning of the Engine-Driver included, not only the words which the unfortunate Signalman had repeated to me as haunting him, but also the words which I myself − not he − had attached, and that only in my own mind, to the gesticulation he had imitated.

Gustav Meyrink
DR CINDERELLA'S PLANTS

THAT'S it, over there: that black little bronze between the candlesticks is the cause of all the weird experiences I have undergone in recent years.

All those tell-tale incidents which have steadily been draining away my vitality now fall into place like the links of a chain. A chain which, when retraced into the past, always leads back to one and the same starting point: that little bronze statuette.

Even if I pretend that there are other explanations, that object looms into view like a milestone by the roadside. And where the road leads — whether to the light of understanding, or to ever greater horrors — is something I would rather not know. Better to make the most of the brief respite which fate has granted me before the next trauma.

I dug it up, quite accidentally, when poking about with my stick in the desert sands at Thebes. The moment I examined it more closely, I was filled with a morbid curiosity, an urge to discover what it actually meant. I, who had never before displayed anything like a thirst for knowledge!

At first, I asked all manner of experts about it, but without success. There was one famous Arabian collector, though, who probably came nearest the mark:

'An imitation of an Egyptian hieroglyph,' he supposed, adding that the figure's strangely clasped hands were sure to indicate some sort of state of ecstasy.

I took the statuette with me to Europe and scarcely an evening can have gone by without my pondering over its mysterious significance, delving into the strangest of thoughts.

A terrible feeling came over me: that I was dealing with something venomous, something malevolent, which, with an artful complacence, was allowing itself to be released from the spell of lifelessness in order to attach itself to me like some incurable disease, thereafter to remain the shadowy tyrant of my life. Then, one day, I had a flash of inspiration that solved the riddle for me. The answer came to me so suddenly, and with such force, that it left me completely stunned.

These sudden insights streak across our inner lives like meteors. We have no idea where they come from: we only see them glow white hot, then fall out of sight. The feeling is almost one of fear... just as if some stranger — but what was I going to say! Forgive me, I am sometimes strangely absent-minded these days, ever since I have had to drag along behind me this palsied left leg of mine. Yes, indeed; the answer I had been seeking was suddenly staring me in the face: *imitate!*

It was as though the word had smashed through a dam wall, releasing a flood of realization: *this* was the one and only key to all the riddles of our earthly existence.

Secret, automatic imitation; unconscious and unremitting — the hidden pilot of all creatures! The all-powerful, mysterious pilot, the masked helmsman who, in the half-light of its dawn, silently boards the ship of life. From out of the chasms where our souls will wander when deep sleep has

...where our souls will wander when deep sleep has shut the gates of day.

shut the gates of day. Perhaps, down there, deep in the crevices of corporal being, lies the archetype of some demon who demands that we imitate his image...

That one word 'imitate', that laconic exhortation from 'somewhere', became a journey on which I immediately embarked.

I stood up, raised both arms above my head, like the statue, and held my fingers downwards with the nails touching the top of my head.

Gustav Meyrink

But nothing happened. There was no change, either internal or external.

To make sure I had got the posture right, I took a closer look at the figure, whereupon I noted that its eyes were shut as if it were asleep. That was enough for me. I gave up, and waited for night to fall. Then I stopped the ticking of the clock, lay down, and again took up the same position of arms and hands.

Several minutes passed, but I am sure I did not fall asleep. Suddenly, it seemed as though a rumbling sound were emanating from deep inside of me, like the noise of a large rock rolling into an abyss.

Then it was as if my own consciousness went tumbling after it, down an endless flight of steps, leaping two at a time, then four, then eight, in ever-increasing jumps. Thus proceeded the jerky descent of my consciousness of life, until a phantasm of death came over me.

What happened then, I will not recount; no one will tell of it.

True, people laugh at the magic secret of the Egyptians and the Chaldeans, guarded by sacred vipers; a secret which not one of the thousands of those initiated ever betrayed.

We should say that no oath on earth might bind so surely!

I used to be of the same opinion, but at that instant I understood everything. For it is not a question of human experience, where the things we perceive are consecutive; nor is it an oath which binds the tongue. It is no more than the mere hint of those things here — here on this earth. Then those vipers make straight for your heart.

That is why the great secret is kept: because it keeps itself. And a secret it will remain until the end of time.

But all this is connected only indirectly with that searing experience from which I shall never recover. A man's outward fate, too, veers onto a new course, when once his consciousness has broken even for an instant through the barrier of earthly cognition.

A fact of which I am living proof.

From that night on which I stepped out of my body, for I can scarcely refer to it otherwise, the course of my life was changed. My once peaceful existence now meanders from one enigmatic, horrific experience to the next — on the way to some dark, unknown destination.

It is as if some demonic hand were allocating me ever shorter intervals of respite between the more and more terrifying hallucinations it sends my way. As though it wished to drive me to a new, unknown form of madness

– gradually, and with extreme meticulousness. To the sort of madness which no one else might notice or suspect, of which only I, afflicted with nameless torments, am aware.

Within days of that experiment with the hieroglyph, I began to perceive things which I considered at first to be no more than delusions of my senses. I heard extraneous tones, strangely droning or whining, cut through the hubbub of everyday life. I saw brilliant colours which had not been there before. Mysterious creatures would suddenly emerge in front of me, inaudible and to others invisible; they would perform incomprehensible and apparently aimless actions. So, for example, they were able to transform themselves, then suddenly lie still, as if they were dead. Then they might merge, like slimy threads hanging down from the gutters, or squat with imbecilic lassitude in the dark passageways between the houses.

This state of heightened perception is not permanent: it waxes and wanes like the moon. But my increasing disinterest in humanity, whose hopes and desires seem far removed from me, shows me that my soul is ever on some dark journey, a long, long way from humanity.

At first I let myself be led by the persuasive feeling which filled me. But now I am like a horse in harness, and I *must* tread the paths along which it leads me.

And there you are: one night it dragged me out, took me to wander aimlessly through the still streets of the Little Quarter, on account of the fantastic aspect presented by the antique houses there.

There is no place on earth more terrifying than that district of Prague. It is never quite dark there, and never quite light. From somewhere up on the hill where the Hradčany castle stands, a dim, lack-lustre beam of light stretches downwards onto the rooftops like so much phosphorescent vapour. Then you turn off into some little street where there is only a lifeless gloom – until an eerie ray of light springs from a crack between shutters, stabbing at your pupils like some malevolent needle.

A house emerges from the mist, a house with crooked shoulders and a receding forehead; it is as soulless as a dead animal, its dormer-windows gaping up at the night sky. The one next door cranes over, peering through its lighted windows to see if the goldsmith's child, drowned a hundred years, is still lying at the bottom of the well. And if you walk along the lumpy cobblestones and look around suddenly, you would swear you had seen a pale, pocked face dart back behind the corner, but not at shoulder height.

No, this face was quite low down — about where a large dog might have its head...

There was not a soul abroad that night. All was as silent as the tomb. The ancient gates of the houses silently pursed their lips.

I turned into Thun Street, where the palace of Countess Mořínová stands. There a narrow house crouched in the fog, only a couple of window-lengths wide, a jumble of hectic, evil-looking masonry. I was

...a pale, pocked face... behind the corner... about where a large dog might have its head...

constrained to stop in front of it, and I could feel that state of heightened perception coming over me.

When that happens, I act with the speed of lightning, as if governed by some outside will; I scarcely know what the next instant will require me to do. So it was that I leaned against an unlocked door, and strode along a passageway and down some steps into a cellar, as if I were at home in the house. It was then that the invisible bridle which leads me about like an obedient animal released me again, and I stood there in the dark, tortured by the awareness that I had acted quite irrationally.

Why had I gone in? Why had it never even occurred to me to resist such a stupid idea? I was clearly ill, and felt relieved that there was no more to it than that ghastly invisible hand.

But then I realized that I had opened the door, entered the house and descended the steps without once faltering, just as if I knew my way around there, and my heart sank.

Gradually, my eyes grew accustomed to the gloom, and I was able to survey my environs.

Someone was sitting on one of the cellar steps. Strange, that I had not bumped into him as I passed! In the darkness, I could only dimly discern the hunched figure. A black beard stood out against a bare chest. The arms, too, were bare. Only the legs were covered by a pair of trousers, or some other sort of cloth. The hands had a terrifying appearance — they were bent back grotesquely, almost at right-angles to the wrists.

For a long time I stood staring at the man. He was deathly still, so that his outline seemed to grow out of the dark background, as if he was doomed to remain there until the house itself fell down.

My skin crawled with horror, and I crept further along the winding passage. At one point I felt for the wall, and my fingers alighted on an open wooden lattice, like those used for training climbing plants. And it was thickly overgrown — so much so that I almost got caught up in the fleshy tendrils. But I could not understand why those plants, or whatever they were, were warm to the touch, and somehow swollen. They had a strangely animal feel to them.

I put my hand out again, but this time I snatched it back with a start. I had touched a round object about the size of a walnut, which felt cold and leapt away from me at once.

Was it a beetle?

At that moment a light shone out, illuminating the wall in front of me.

All the fear and horror I have ever felt in my life dwindled into triviality compared to that moment. Every sinew in my body started to tremble with indescribable terror. A silent scream from my paralysed voice sent an icy shiver through me.

From floor to ceiling the wall was covered in bloody veins, from which hundreds of goggling eyes hung like strawberries. The one I had just

Gustav Meyrink

touched was still moving jerkily back and forth and peering at me resentfully.

I felt close to collapse, but managed to take a couple more steps along the passage. I was met by a cloud of unpleasant odours, among them the stench of something decaying, of rotten vegetables, something between fungus and mulberries. My knees began to shake, and I struck out on all sides. Just then a sort of glowing ring caught my eye — it was the wick of an oil lamp which was about to go out. It gave another flicker of life: I leapt towards it, and with trembling flingers turned the wick up to save it from extinguishment.

I then turned round in a single movement, holding the lamp in front of me like a sort of shield. The space in which I was standing was empty. On the table where the lamp had been lay an elongated, shiny object.

I reached out instinctively in order to acquire a weapon, but I found myself holding only something light and somewhat prickly.

Nothing moved, and I sighed with relief. Cautiously, afraid of quenching the flame, I shone the lamp along the wall. Everywhere I saw the same wooden espaliers, interwoven, as I had already seen only too well, with what were apparently many veins joined together and pulsating with blood. Among them countless eyeballs glimmered ghoulishly, their sickening, bilberry-like pupils slowly turning to watch me as I passed. Eyes of all sizes and colours, from those with sparkling iridescence to a light blue horse's eye which gazed motionlessly up at the ceiling.

Many of them were wrinkled and black, and looked like withered deadly nightshade berries.

The chief arteries were growing out of blood-filled flasks which somehow kept them supplied with liquid. I stumbled against a bowl, and found it to be filled with lumps of whitish fat, out of which toadstools were growing, their heads covered in a vitreous skin; pink-fleshed toadstools which shrank at the merest touch.

Everything seemed to have been put together by some incomprehensible art from parts of living bodies, deprived of their human souls and constrained to a mere vegetable existence. But alive they were: that I knew, for when I had shone the light in those eyes the pupils had contracted at once. What fiendish gardener could have planted this monstrous plot?

I recalled the figure on the cellar steps. Instinctively, I reached into my pocket in search of a weapon of some sort, and my fingers closed on the scaly object I had put there a moment earlier.

It was like a pinkish, opalescent pine-cone, and I now realized that it was made of human fingernails. With a shudder of horror, I let it fall to the ground, and gritted my teeth: I must get out of here at once, even if the creature on the steps were to come to life and hurl himself upon me!

In seconds I had reached the stairway, ready to attack first. But I saw now that the fellow was dead. He was the colour of sallow wax. From the fingers of his clasped hands the nails had been torn, and neat incisions in his

Just like the Egyptian hieroglyph; the same stance, the same gesture!

chest and temples revealed that an autopsy had been performed. As I hurried past him my hand must have brushed against his body, for it slipped down a couple of steps and suddenly stood there upright, the arms raised and turned inwards, the fingers resting on the crown of the head.

Just like the Egyptian hieroglyph; the same stance, the same gesture!

Then I remember only that the lamp shattered and I flung open the door into the street, where I felt the demon palsy grip my thumping heart in its cold fingers. In the state of half-awareness that ensued, I realized that the fellow on the steps must have been suspended by cords tied at the elbows, so that the body was jerked upright as it fell down the stairs... then... then a distant-sounding voice said: 'You're to go in to see the Commissioner now.'

I entered a poorly-lit room with long pipes standing beside the wall and a uniform coat hanging from a stand. It was the Police Commissioner's office.

A constable was holding me up. The Commissioner sat at a desk, and he kept looking at something behind me. 'Any identification?' he muttered.

'He had some visiting-cards. We took them off him,' I heard the constable reply.

'What were you doing in Thun Street in front of an open door?'

There was a long pause.

'You!' snapped the constable, giving me a sharp nudge.

I blurted out something about murder in a cellar on Thun Street. The constable left the room. With his eyes still fixed on a point behind my back, the Commissioner uttered a long sentence. All I could make out was: 'Whatever do you mean? Doctor Cinderella is a most learned man — an egyptologist. He grows all manner of new, carnivorous plants — *Nepenthe*, *Drosera* and whatnot — I'm not quite sure... you should stay at home at night.'

At that moment the door behind me creaked open. I turned, and saw a tall creature with a heron's beak standing there: it was the Egyptian Anubis.

My vision grew clouded. Anubis bowed to the Commissioner, walked up to me, and whispered: 'Doctor Cinderella — at your service.'

Doctor Cinderella!

At that moment I remembered something important from the past — something I forgot again instantly.

When I looked at Anubis again, he had turned into a clerk; only his nose was beak-like. He handed me my own visiting-cards, with the name *Doctor Cinderella* written on them.

The Commissioner looked at me suddenly, and I heard him say: 'Why, it's you, Doctor. You ought to stay at home at night.'

The clerk led me out. On the way I stumbled slightly, and knocked against the coat on the stand.

It slid slowly off the peg, and was left hanging by the arms. I watched its shadow on the wall as it raised its arms above its head and moronically took up the posture of the Egyptian statue.

Well, there you are — that was my last 'event'. Since then I have been paralysed: the two halves of my face are different, and I drag my left leg along behind me. But I have not been able to find that little house again, and no one at the police station remembers anything of what happened that night.

...he had turned into a clerk; only his nose was beak-like.

Sir Edward Bulwer-Lytton
THE HAUNTED HOUSE

A FRIEND of mine, who is a man of letters and a philosopher, said to me one day, as if between jest and earnest: 'Fancy! Since last we met, I have discovered a haunted house in the midst of London.'

'Really haunted? – And by what? Ghosts?'

'Well, I can't answer that question; all I know is this – six weeks ago my wife and I were in search of a furnished apartment. Passing a quiet street, we saw on the window of one of the houses a bill, "Apartments Furnished."

'...I have discovered a haunted house in the midst of London.'

The situation suited us; we entered the house – liked the rooms – engaged them by the week – and left them the third day. No power on earth could have reconciled my wife to stay longer; and I don't wonder at it.'

'What did you see?'

'Excuse me – I have no desire to be ridiculed as a superstitious dreamer – nor, on the other hand, could I ask you to accept on my affirmation what you would hold to be incredible without the evidence of your own senses. Let me only say this, it is not so much what we saw or heard (in which you might fairly suppose that we were the dupes of our own excited fancy, or the victims of imposture in others), that drove us away, as it was an undefinable terror which seized both of us whenever we passed by the door of a certain unfurnished room, in which we neither saw nor heard anything. And the strangest marvel of all was, that for once in my life I agreed with my wife, silly woman though she be — and allowed, after the third night, that it was impossible to stay a fourth in that house. Accordingly, on the fourth morning, I summoned the woman who kept the house and attended on us, and told her that the rooms did not quite suit us, and we could not stay out our week. She said, dryly, 'I know why; you have stayed longer than any other lodger. Few ever stayed a second night; none before you a third. But I take it they have been very kind to you.'

'They — who?' I asked, affecting a smile.

'Why, they who haunt the house, whoever they are. I don't mind them; I remember them many years ago, when I lived in this house, not as a servant; but I know they will be the death of me some day. I don't care — I'm old, and must die soon anyhow; and then I shall be with them, and in this house still.' The woman spoke with so dreary a sadness, that really it was a sort of awe that prevented my conversing with her further. I paid for my week, and too happy were I and my wife to get off so cheaply.'

'You excite my curiosity,' said I; 'nothing I should like better than to sleep in a haunted house. Pray give me the address of the one which you left so ignominously.'

My friend gave me the address; and when we parted, I walked straight towards the house thus indicated.

It is situated on the north side of Oxford Street, in a dull but respectable thoroughfare. I found the house shut up — no bill at the window, and no response to my knock. As I was turning away, a beer boy, collecting pewter pots at the neighbouring areas, said to me: 'Do you want anyone at that house, sir?'

'Yes, I heard it was to be let.'

'Let! — why, the woman who kept it is dead — has been dead these three weeks, and no one can be found to stay there, though Mr J-- offered ever so much. He offered mother, who chars for him, £1 a week just to open and shut the windows, and she would not.'

'Would not! — and why?'

'The house is haunted; and the old woman who kept it was found dead in her bed, with her eyes wide open. They say the devil strangled her.'

'Pooh! — you speak of Mr J--. Is he the owner of the house?'

'Yes.'

'Where does he live?'

'In G-- Street, No.--.'

'What is he? − in any business?'

'No sir − nothing particular; a single gentleman.'

I gave the pot-boy the gratuity earned by his liberal information, and proceeded to Mr J--, in G--Street, which was close by the street that boasted the haunted house. I was lucky enough to find Mr J-- at home − an elderly man, with intelligent countenance and preposessing manners.

I communicated my name and my business frankly. I said I heard the house was considered to be haunted − that I had a strong desire to examine a house with so equivocal a reputation − that I should be greatly obliged if he would allow me to hire it, though only for a night. I was willing to pay for that privilege whatever he might be inclined to ask. 'Sir,' said Mr J--, with great courtesy, 'the house is at your service, for as short or as long a time as you please. Rent is out of the question − the obligation will be on my side should you be able to discover the cause of the strange phenomena which at present deprive it of all value. I cannot let it, for I cannot even get a servant to keep it in order or answer the door. Unluckily the house is haunted, if I may use that expression, not only by night, but by day; though at night the disturbances are of a more unpleasant and sometimes of a more alarming character. The poor old woman who died in it three weeks ago was a pauper whom I took out of a work-house, for in her childhood she had been known to some of my family, and had once been in such good circumstances that she had rented that house of my uncle. She was a woman of superior education and strong mind, and was the only person I could ever induce to remain in the house. Indeed, since her death, which was sudden, and the coroner's inquest, which gave it a notoriety in the neighbourhood, I have so despaired of finding any person to take charge of the house, much more a tenant, that I would willingly let it rent-free for a year to anyone who would pay its rates and taxes.'

'How long is it since the house acquired this sinister character?'

'That I can scarcely tell you, but very many years since. The old woman I spoke of said it was haunted when she rented it between thirty and forty years ago. The fact is, that my life has been spent in the East Indies, and in the civil service of the Company. I returned to England last year, on inheriting the fortune of an uncle, among whose possession was the house in question. I found it shut up, and uninhabited. I was told that it was haunted, that no one would inhabit. I smiled at what seemed to me so idle a story. I spent some money in repairing it − added to its old-fashion furniture a few modern articles − advertised it, and obtained a lodger for a year. He was a colonel retired on half-pay. He came in with his family, a son and a daughter, and four or five servants; they all left the house the next day; and although each of them declared that he had seen something different from that which had scared the others, a something still was equally terrible to all. I really could not in conscience sue, nor even blame, the colonel for breach of agreement. Then I put in the old woman I have spoken of, and she was empowered to let the house in apartments. I never had one lodger who stayed more than three days. I do not tell you their stories − to no two lodgers have there been exactly the same phenomena repeated. It is better that you should judge for yourself, than enter the house with an imagination influenced by previous narratives; only be prepared to see and to hear something or other, and take what ever precaution you yourself please.'

'Had you never a curiosity yourself to pass a night in that house?'

'Yes. I passed not a night, but three hours in broad daylight in that house. My curiosity is not satisfied, but it is quenched. I have no desire to renew the experiment. You cannot complain, you see, sir, that I am not sufficiently candid; and unless your interest be exceedingly eager, and your nerves unusually strong, I honestly add, that I advise you *not* to pass a night in that house.'

'My interest is exceedingly keen,' said I, 'and though only a coward will boast of his nerves in situations wholly unfamiliar to him, yet my nerves have been seasoned in such variety of danger that I have the right to rely on them − even in a haunted house.'

Mr J-- said very little more; he took the keys of the house out of his bureau, gave them to me, and thanking him cordially for his frankness, and his urbane concession to my wish, I carried off my prize.

Impatient for the experiment, as soon as I reached home, I summoned my confidential servant − a young man of gay spirits, fearless temper, and as free from superstitious prejudice as anyone I could think of.

'F--,' said I, 'you remember in Germany how disappointed we were at not finding a ghost in that old castle, which was said to be haunted by a headless apparition? Well, I have heard of a house in London which, I have reason to hope, is decidedly haunted. I mean to sleep there tonight. From what I hear, there is no doubt that something will allow itself to be seen or to be heard − something, perhaps, excessively horrible. Do you think, if I take you with me, I may rely on your presence of mind, whatever may happen?'

'Oh, sir! pray trust me,' answered F--, grinning with delight.

'Very well; then here are the keys of the house — this is the address. Go now — select for me any bedroom you please; and since the house has not been inhabited for weeks, make up a good fire — air the bed well — see, of course, that there are candles as well as fuel. Take with you my revolver and my dagger — so much for my weapons — arm yourself equally well! and if we are not a match for a dozen ghosts, we shall be but a sorry couple of Englishmen.'

I was engaged for the rest of the day on business so urgent that I had not leisure to think much on the nocturnal adventure to which I had plighted my honour. I dined alone, and very late, and while dining, read, as is my habit. I selected one of the volumes of Macaulay's Essays. I thought to myself that I would take the book with me; there was so much of healthfulness in the style, and practical life in the subjects, that it would serve as an antidote against the influences of superstitious fancy.

Accordingly, about half-past nine, I put the book into my pocket, and strolled leisurely towards the haunted house. I took with me a favourite dog — an exceedingly sharp, bold, and vigilant bull-terrier — a dog fond of prowling about strange ghostly corners and passages at night in search of rats — a dog of dogs for a ghost.

It was a summer night, but chilly, the sky somewhat gloomy and overcast. Still there was a moon — faint and sickly, but still a moon — and if the clouds permitted, after midnight it would be brighter.

I reached the house, knocked, and my servant opened with a cheerful smile.

'All right, sir, and very comfortable.'

'Oh!' said I, rather disappointed; 'have you not seen or heard anything remarkable?'

'Well, sir, I must own I have heard something queer.'

'What? — what?'

'The sound of feet pattering behind me; and once or twice small noises like whispers close at my ear — nothing more.'

'You are not at all frightened?'

'I! not a bit of it, sir;' and the man's bold look reassured me on one point — viz., that, happen what might, he would not desert me.

We were in the hall, the street door closed, and my attention was now drawn to my dog. He had at first run in eagerly enough, but had sneaked back to the door, and was scratching and whining to get out. After patting him on the head, and encouraging him gently, the dog seemed to reconcile himself to the situation, and followed me and F-- through the house, but keeping close at my heels instead of hurrying inquisitively in advance, which was his usual and normal habit in all strange places. We first visited the subterranean apartments, the kitchen and other offices, and especially the cellars, in which last there were two or three bottles of wine still left in a bin, covered with cobwebs, and, evidently, by their appearance, undisturbed for many years. It was clear that the ghosts were not winebibbers. For the rest we discovered nothing of interest. There was a gloomy, little back-yard, with very high walls. The stones of this yard were very damp; and what with the damp, and what with the dust and smoke-grime on the pavement, our feet left a slight impression where we passed. And now appeared the first strange phenomenon witnessed by myself in this strange abode. I saw, just before me, the print of a foot suddenly form itself, as it were. I stopped, caught hold of my servant, and pointed to it. In advance of the footprint as suddenly dropped another. We both saw it. I advanced quickly to the place, the footprint kept advancing before me, a small footprint − the foot of a child; the impression was too faint thoroughly to distinguish the shape, but it seemed to us both that it was the print of a naked foot. This phenomenon ceased when we arrived at the opposite wall, nor did it repeat itself on returning. We remounted the stairs, and entered the rooms on the ground floor, a dining parlour, a small back parlour, and a still smaller third room that had been probably appropriated to a footman − all still as death. We then visited the drawing-rooms, which seemed fresh and new. In the front room I seated myself in the arm-chair. F-- placed on the table the candlestick with which he had lighted us. I told him to shut the door. As he turned to do so, a chair opposite to me moved from the wall quickly and noiselessly, and dropped itself about a yard from my own chair, immediately fronting it.

'Why, this is better than the turning-tables,' said I, with a half-laugh; and as I laughed, my dog put back his head and howled.

F--, coming back, had not observed the movement of the chair. He employed himself now in stilling the dog. I continued to gaze on the chair, and fancied I saw on it a pale, blue, misty outline of a human figure, but an outline so indistinct that I could only distrust my own vision. The dog now was quiet. 'Put back that chair opposite to me,' said I to F--: 'put it back to the wall.'

F-- obeyed. 'Was that you, sir?' said he, turning abruptly.

'I! — what?'

'Why, something struck me. I felt it sharply on the shoulder — just here.'

'No,' said I. 'But we have jugglers present, and though we may not discover their tricks, we shall catch *them* before they frighten *us*.'

We did not stay long in the drawing-rooms — in fact, they felt so damp and so chilly that I was glad to get to the fire upstairs. We locked the doors of the drawing-rooms — a precaution which, I should observe, we had taken with all the rooms we had searched below. The bedroom my servant had selected for me was the best on the floor — a large one, with two windows fronting the street. The four-posted bed, which took up no inconsiderable space, was opposite to the fire, which burned clear and bright; a door in the wall to the left, between the bed and the window, communicated with the room which my servant appropriated to himself. This last was a small room with a sofa-bed, and had no communication with the landing-place — no other door but that which conducted to the bedroom I was to occupy. On either side of my fireplace was a cupboard, without locks, flush with the wall, and covered with the same dull-brown paper. We examined these cupboards — only hooks to suspend female dresses — nothing else; we sounded the walls — evidently solid — the outer walls of the building. Having finished the survey of these apartments, warmed myself a few moments, and lighted my cigar, I then, still accompanied by F--, went forth to complete my reconnoitre. In the landing-place there was another door; it was closed firmly. 'Sir,' said my servant, in surprise, 'I unlocked this door with all the others when I first came; it cannot have got locked from the inside, for--'

Before he had finished his sentence, the door, which neither of us then was touching, opened quietly of itself. We looked at each other an instant. The same thought seized both — some human agency might be detected here. I rushed in first, my servant followed. A small, blank, dreary room without furniture — a few empty boxes and hampers in a corner — a small window — the shutters closed — not even a fireplace — no other door but that by which we had entered — no carpet on the floor, and the floor seemed very old, uneven, worm-eaten, mended here and there, as was shown by the whiter patches on the wood; but no living being, and no visible place in which a living being could have hidden. As we stood gazing around, the door by which we had entered closed as quietly as it had before opened; we were imprisoned.

E. Bulwer-Lytton

For the first time I felt a creep of undefinable horror. Not so my servant. 'Why, they don't think to trap us, sir; I could break that trumpery door with a kick of my foot.'

'Try first if it will open to your hand,' said I, shaking off the vague apprehension that had seized me, 'while I unclose the shutters and see what is without.'

I unbarred the shutters — the window looked on the little backyard I have before described; there was no ledge without — nothing to break the sheer descent of the wall. No man getting out of that window would have found any footing till he had fallen on the stones below.

F--, meanwhile, was vainly attempting to open the door. He now turned round to me, and asked my permission to use force. And I should here state, in justice to the servant, that, far from evincing any superstitious terrors, his nerve, composure, and even gaiety amidst circumstances so extraordinary, compelled my admiration, and made me congratulate myself on having secured a companion in every way fitted to the occasion. I willingly gave him the permission he required. But though he was a remarkably strong man, his force was as idle as his milder efforts; the door did not even shake to his stoutest kick. Breathless and panting, he desisted. I then tried the door myself, equally in vain. As I ceased from the effort, again that creep of horror came over me; but this time it was more cold and stubborn. I felt as if some strange and ghastly exhalation were rising up from the chinks of that rugged floor, and filling the atmosphere with a venomous influence hostile to human life. The door now very slowly and quietly opened as if of its own accord. We precipitated ourselves into the landing-place. We both saw a large, pale light — as large as the human figure, but shapeless and unsubstantial — move before us, and ascend the stairs that led from the landing into the attics. I followed the light, and my servant followed me. It entered, to the right of the landing, a small garret, of which the door stood open. I entered in the same instant. The light then collapsed into a small globule, exceedingly brilliant and vivid; rested a moment on a bed in the corner, quivered and vanished. We approached the bed and examined it — a half-tester, such as is commonly found in attics devoted to servants. On the drawers that stood near it were perceived an old, faded silk kerchief, with the needle still left in a rent half repaired. The kerchief was covered with dust; probably it had belonged to the old woman who had last died in that house, and this might have been her sleeping-room. I had sufficient curiosity to open the drawers; there were a few odds and ends of female dress, and two letters tied round with a narrow ribbon of faded yellow. I took the liberty to possess myself of the letters. We found nothing else in the room worth noticing – nor did the light reappear; but we distinctly heard, as we turned to go, a pattering footfall on the floor – just before us. We went through the other attics (in all four), the footfall still preceding us. Nothing to be seen – nothing but the footfall heard. I had the letters in my hand; just as I was descending the stairs I distinctly felt my wrist seized, and a faint, soft effort made to draw the letters from my clasp. I only held them the more tightly, and the effort ceased.

We regained the bedchamber appropriated to myself, and I then remarked that my dog had not followed us when we had left it.

He was thrusting himself close to the fire, and trembling. I was impatient to examine the letters; and while I read them, my servant opened a little box in which he had deposited the weapons I had ordered him to bring, took them out, placed them on a table close to my bed-head, and then occupied himself in soothing the dog, who, however, seemed to heed him very little.

The letters were short – they were dated; the dates exactly thirty-five years ago. They were evidently from a lover to his mistress, or a husband to some young wife. Not only the terms of expression, but a distinct reference to a former voyage, indicated the writer to have been a seafarer. The spelling and hand-writing were those of a man imperfectly educated, but still the language itself was forcible. In the expressions of endearment there was a kind of rough, wild love; but here and there were dark unintelligible hints at some secret not of love – some secret that seemed of crime. 'We ought to love each other,' was one of the sentences I remember, 'for how everyone else would execrate us if all was known.' Again: 'Don't let anyone be in the same room with you at night – you talk in your sleep.' And again: 'what's done can't be undone; and I tell you there's nothing against us unless the dead could come to life.' Here there was underlined in a better handwriting (a female's), 'They do!' At the end of the letter latest in date the same female hand had written these words: 'Lost at sea the 4th of June, the same day as--'

I put down the letters, and began to muse over their contents.

Fearing, however, that the train of thoughts into which I fell might unsteady my nerves, I fully determined to keep my mind in a fit state to cope with whatever of marvellous the advancing night might bring forth. I roused myself − laid the letters on the table − stirred up the fire, which was still bright and cheering − and opened my volume of Macaulay. I read quietly enough until about half-past eleven. I then threw myself dressed upon the bed, and told my servant he might retire to his own room, but must keep himself awake. I bade him leave open the door between the two rooms. Thus alone, I kept two candles burning on the table by my bed-head. I laced my watch beside the weapons, and calmly resumed my Macaulay. Opposite to me the fire burned clear; and on the hearth-rug, seemingly asleep, lay the dog. In about twenty minutes I felt an exceedingly cold air pass by my cheek, like a sudden draught. I fancied the door to my right, communicating with the landing-place, must have got open; but no − it was closed. I then turned my glance to my left and saw the flame of the candles violently swayed as by a wind. At the same moment the watch beside the revolver softly slid from the table − softly, softly − no visible hand − it was gone. I sprang up, seizing the revolver with one hand, the dagger with the other: I was not willing that my weapons should share the fate of the watch. Thus armed I looked round the floor − no sign of the watch. Three slow, loud, distinct knocks were now heard at the bed-head; my servant called out, 'Is that you, sir?'

'No; be on your guard.'

The dog now roused himself and sat on his haunches, his ears moving quickly backwards and forwards. He kept his eyes fixed on me with a look so strange that he concentrated all attention on himself. Slowly he rose up, all his hair bristling, and stood perfectly rigid, and with the same wild stare. I had no time, however, to examine the dog. Presently my servant emerged from his room; and if ever I saw horror in the human face, it was then. I should not have recognized him had we met in the street, so altered was every lineament. He passed by me quickly, saying in a whisper that seemed scarcely to come from his lips. 'Run − run! it is after me!' He gained the door to the landing, pulled it open, and rushed forth. I followed him into the landing involuntarily, calling to him to stop: but, without heeding me, he bounded down the stairs, clinging to the balusters, and taking several steps at a time. I heard, where I stood, the street-door open − heard it again clap to. I was left alone in the haunted house.

It was but for a moment that I remained undecided whether or not to follow my servant; pride and curiosity alike forbade so dastardly a flight. I re-entered my room, closing the door after me, and proceeded cautiously into the interior chamber. I encountered nothing to justify my servant's

terror. I again carefully examined the walls, to see if there were any
concealed door. I could find no trace of one — not even a seam in the
dull-brown paper with which the room was hung. How then, had the THING,
whatever it was, which had so scared him, obtained ingress except through
my own chamber?

I returned to my room, shut and locked the door that opened upon the
interior one, and stood on the hearth, expectant and prepared. I now

...the dog had slunk into an angle of the wall...

perceived that the dog had slunk into an angle of the wall, and was pressing
himself close against it, as if literally striving to force his way into it.
I approached the animal and spoke to it; the poor brute was evidently
beside itself with terror. It showed all its teeth, the saliva dropping from its
jaws, and would certainly have bitten me if I had touched it. It did not seem
to recognize me. Whoever has seen at the Zoological Gardens a rabbit
fascinated by a serpent, cowering in a corner, may form some idea of the

anguish which the dog exhibited. Finding all efforts to soothe the animal in vain, and fearing that his bite might be as venomous in that state as in the madness of hydrophobia, I left him alone, placed my weapons on the table beside the fire, seated myself, and re-commenced my Macaulay.

Perhaps, in order not to appear seeking credit for a courage, or rather a coolness, which the reader may conceive I exaggerate, I may be pardoned if I pause to indulge in one or two egotistical remarks.

As I hold presence of mind, or what is called courage, to be precisely proportioned to familiarity with the circumstances that lead to it, so I should say that I had been long sufficiently familiar with all experiments that appertain to the Marvellous. I had witnessed many very extraordinary phenomena that would be either totally disbelieved if I stated them, or ascribed to supernatural agencies. Now, my theory is that the Supernatural is the Impossible, and that what is called supernatural is only a something in the laws of nature, of which we have been hitherto ignorant. Therefore, if a ghost rise before me, I have not the right to say, 'So, then, the supernatural is possible,' but rather, 'So, then, the apparition of a ghost is, contrary to received opinion, within the laws of nature − *i. e.* not supernatural.

Now, in all that I had hitherto witnessed, and, indeed, in all the wonders which the amateurs of mystery in our age record as facts, a material living agency is always required. On the Continent you will find still magicians who assert that they can raise spirits. Assume for the moment that they assert truly, still the living material form of the magician is present; and he is the material agency by which, from some constitutional peculiarities, certain strange phenomena are represented to your natural senses.

Accept, again, as truthful the tales of Spirit Manifestation in America − musical or other sounds − writings on paper, produced by no discernable hand − articles of furniture moved without apparent human agency − or the actual sight and touch of hands, to which no bodies seem to belong − still there must be found the MEDIUM or living being, with constitutional peculiarities capable of obtaining these signs. In fine, in all such marvels, supposing even that there is no imposture there must be a human being like ourselves, by whom, or through whom, the effects presented to human beings are produced. It is so with the now familiar phenomena of mesmerism or electro-biology; the mind of the person operated on is affected through a material living agent. Nor supposing it true that a mesmerized patient can respond to the will or passes of a mesmerizer a hundred miles distant, is the response less occasioned by a material being, it may be through a material fluid — call it Electric, call it Odic, call it what you will — which has the power of traversing space and passing obstacles, that the material effect is communicated from one to the other. Hence all that I had hitherto witnessed, or expected to witness, in this strange house, I believed to be occasioned through some agency or medium as mortal as myself; and this idea necessarily prevented the awe with which those who regard as supernatural things that are not within the ordinary operation of nature, might have been impressed by the adventures of that memorable night.

As, then, it was my conjecture that all that was presented, or would be presented, to my senses must originate in some human being gifted by constitution with the power so to present them, and having some motive so to do, I felt an interest in my theory which, in its way, was rather philosophical than superstitious. And I can sincerely say that I was in as tranquil a temper for observation as any practical experimentalist could be in awaiting the effects of some rare, though perhaps perilous, chemical combination. Of course, the more I kept my mind detached from fancy, the more the temper fitted for observation would be obtained; and I therefore riveted eye and thought on the strong daylight sense in the page of my Macaulay.

I now became aware that something interposed between the page and the light — the page was over-shadowed; I looked up, and I saw what I shall find it very difficult, perhaps impossible, to describe.

It was a Darkness shaping itself forth from the air in very undefined outline. I cannot say it was of a human form, and yet it had more resemblance to a human form, or rather shadow, than to anything else. As it stood, wholly apart and distinct from the air and the light around it, its dimensions seemed gigantic, the summit nearly touching the ceiling. While I gazed, a feeling of intense cold seized me. An iceberg before me could not more have chilled me; nor could the cold of an iceberg have been more purely physical. I feel convinced that it was not the cold caused by fear. As I continued to gaze, I thought — but this I cannot say with precision — that I distinguished two eyes looking down on me from the height. One moment I fancied that I distinguished them clearly, the next they seemed gone; but still two rays of a pale-blue light frequently shot through the darkness, as from the height on which I half believed, half doubted, that I had encountered the eyes.

I strove to speak — my voice utterly failed me; I could only think to myself, 'Is this fear? it is *not* fear!' I strove to rise — in vain; I felt as if weighed down by an irresistible force. Indeed, my impression was that of an immense and overwhelming Power opposed to my volition; that sense of utter inadequacy to cope with a force beyond man's, which one may feel *physically* in a storm at sea, in a conflagration, or when confronting some terrible wild beast, or rather, perhaps, the shark of the ocean, I felt *morally*. Opposed to my will was another will, as far superior to its strength as storm, fire, and shark are superior in material force to the force of man.

And now, as this impression grew on me — now came, at last, horror — horror to a degree that no words can convey. Still I retained pride, if not courage; and in my own mind I said, 'This is horror, but it is not fear; unless I fear, I cannot be harmed; my reason rejects this thing; it is an illusion — I do not fear.' With a violent effort I succeeded at last in stretching out my hand toward the weapon on the table; as I did so, on the arm and shoulder I received a strange shock, and my arm fell to my side powerless. And now, to add to my horror, the light began slowly to wane from the candles — they were not, as it were, extinguished, but their flame seemed very gradually withdrawn; it was the same with the fire — the light was extracted from the fuel; in a few minutes the room was in utter darkness. The dread that came over me, to be thus in the dark with that dark Thing, whose power was so intensely felt, brought a reaction of nerve. In fact, terror had reached that climax, that either my senses must have deserted me, or I must have burst through the spell. I did burst through it. I found voice, though the voice was a shriek. I remember that I broke forth with words like these — 'I do not fear, my soul does not fear;' and at the same time I found the strength to rise. Still in that profound gloom I rushed to one of the windows — tore aside the curtain — flung open the shutters; my first thought was — LIGHT. And when I saw the moon high, clear and calm, I felt a joy that almost compensated for the previous terror. There, was the moon, there, was also the light from the gas-lamps in the deserted slumberous street. I turned to look back into the room; the moon penetrated its shadow very palely and partially — but still there was light. The dark Thing, whatever it might be, was gone — except that I could yet see a dim shadow, which seemed the shadow of that shade against the opposite wall.

My eye now rested on the table, and from under the table (which was without cloth or cover — an old mahogany round table) there rose a hand, visible as far as the wrist. It was a hand, seemingly, as much of flesh and blood as my own, but the hand of an aged person – lean, wrinkled, small too – a woman's hand. That hand very softly closed on the two letters that lay on the table; hand and letters both vanished. Then there came the same three loud, measured knocks I had heard at the bed-head before this extraordinary drama had commenced.

As those sounds slowly ceased, I felt the whole room vibrate sensibly; and at the far end there rose, as from the floor, sparks or globules like bubbles of light, many-coloured – green, yellow, fire-red, azure. Up and down, to and fro, hither, thither, as tiny Will-o'-the-Wisps, the sparks moved, slow or swift, each at its own caprice. A chair (as in the drawing-room below) was now advanced from the wall without apparent agency, and placed at the opposite side of the table. Suddenly, as forth from the chair, there grew a shape – a woman's shape. It was distinct as a shape of life – ghastly as a shape of death. The face was that of youth, with a strange, mournful beauty; the throat and shoulders were bare, the rest of the form in a loose robe of cloudy white. It began sleeking its long, yellow hair, which fell over its shoulders; its eyes were not turned towards me, but to the door; it seemed listening, watching, waiting. The shadow of the shade in the background grew darker; and again I thought I beheld the eyes gleaming out from the summit of the shadow – eyes fixed upon that shape.

As if from the door, though it did not open, there grew out another shape, equally distinct, equally ghastly – a man's shape – a young man's. It was in the dress of the last century or rather in a likeness of such dress (for both the male shape and the female, though defined, were evidently unsubstantial, impalpable-simulacra-phantasms); and there was something incongruous, grotesque, yet fearful in the contrast between the elaborate finery, the courtly precision of that old-fashioned garb, with its ruffles, and lace, and buckles, and the corpse-like aspect and ghost-like stillness of the flitting wearer. Just as the male shape approached the female, the dark Shadow started from the wall, all three for a moment wrapped in darkness. When the pale light returned, the two phantoms were as if in the grasp of the Shadow that towered between them, and there was a blood-stain on the breast of the female; and the phantom male was leaning on its phantom sword, and blood seemed trickling fast from the ruffles, from the lace; and the darkness of the intermediate Shadow swallowed them up – they were gone. And again the bubbles of light shot, and sailed, and undulated, growing thicker and thicker and more wildly confused in their movements.

The closet door to the right of the fireplace now opened, and from the aperture there came the form of an aged woman. In her hand she held letters — the very letters over which I had seen the Hand close; and behind her I heard a footstep. She turned round as if to listen, and then she opened the letters and seemed to read; and over her shoulder I saw a livid face, the face as of a man long drowned — bloated, bleached — seaweed tangled in its dripping hair; and at her feet lay a form as of a corpse, and beside the corpse

The face was that of youth, with a strange, mournful beauty...

there cowered a child, a miserable, squalid child, with famine in its cheeks and fear in its eyes. And as I looked in the old woman's face, the wrinkles and lines vanished, and it became a face of youth — hard-eyed, stony, but still youth; and the Shadow darted forth, and darkened over these phantoms as it had darkened over the last.

Nothing now was left but the Shadow, and on that my eyes were intently fixed, till again eyes grew out of the Shadow — malignant, serpent eyes. And the bubbles of light again rose and fell, and in their disordered, irregular, turbulent maze, mingled with the wan moonlight. And now from these globules themselves, as from the shell of an egg, monstrous things burst out; the air grew filled with then; larvae so bloodless and so hideous that I can in no way describe them except to remind the reader of the swarming life which the solar microscope brings before the eyes in a drop of water − things transparent, supple, agile, chasing each other, devouring each other − forms like nought ever beheld by the naked eye. As the shapes were without symmetry, so their movements were without order. In their very vagrancies there was no sport; they came round me and round, thicker and faster and swifter, swarming over my head, crawling over my right arm, which was outstretched in involuntary command against all evil beings. Sometimes I felt myself touched, but not by them; invisible hands touched me. Once I felt the clutch as of cold, soft fingers at my throat. I was still equally conscious that if I gave way to fear I should be in bodily peril; and I concentrated all my faculties in the single focus of resisting, stubborn will. And I turned my sight from the Shadow − above all, from those strange, serpent eyes − eyes that had now become distinctly visible. For there, though in nought else around me, I was aware that there was a *WILL,* and a will of intense, creative, working evil, which might crush down my own.

The pale atmosphere in the room began now to redden as if in the air of some near conflagration. The larvae grew lurid as things that live on fire. Again the room vibrated; again were heard the three measured knocks; and again all things were swallowed up in the darkness of the dark Shadow, as if out of that darkness all had come, into that darkness all returned.

As the gloom receded, the Shadow was wholly gone. Slowly as it had been withdrawn, the flame grew again into the candles on the table, again into the fuel in the grate.

The whole room came once more calmly, healthfully into sight.

The two doors were still closed, the door communicating with the servants' room still locked. In the corner of the wall, into which he had so convulsively niched himself, lay the dog. I called to him − no movement: I approached − the animal was dead; his eyes protruded; his tongue out of his mouth, the froth gathered round his jaws. I took him in my arms; I brought him to the fire; I felt acute grief for the loss of my poor favourite − acute self-reproach; I accused myself of his death, I imagined he had died of fright. But what was my surprise on finding that his neck was actually broken. Had this been done in the dark? − must it not have been by a hand human as mine? − must there not have been a human agency all the while in that room? Good cause to suspect it. I cannot tell. I cannot do more than state the fact fairly; the reader may draw his own inference.

Another surprising circumstance — my watch was restored to the table from which it had been so mysteriously withdrawn; but it had stopped at the very moment it was so withdrawn; nor, despite all the skill of the watchmaker, has it ever gone since — that is, it will go in a strange, erratic way for a few hours, and then come to a dead stop — it is worthless.

Nothing more chanced for the rest of the night. Nor, indeed, had I long to wait before the dawn broke.

Not till it was broad daylight did I quit the haunted house. Before I did so, I revisited the little blind room in which my servant and myself had been for a time imprisoned. I had a strong impression — for which I could not account — that from that room had originated the mechanism of the phenomena — if I may use the term — which had been experienced in my chamber. And though I entered it now in the clear day, with the sun peering through the filmy window, I still felt, as I stood on its floor, the creep of the horror which I had first there experienced the night before, and which had been so aggravated by what had passed in my own chamber. I could not, indeed, bear to stay more than half a minute within those walls. I descended the stairs, and again I heard the footfall before me; and when I opened the street door, I thought I could distinguish a very low laugh. I gained my own home, expecting to find my runaway servant there. But he had not presented himself; nor did I hear more of him for three days, when I received a letter from him, dated from Liverpool, to this effect:

'HONOURED SIR, — I humbly entreat your pardon, though I can scarcely hope that you will think I deserve it, unless — which Heaven forbid! — you saw what I did. I feel that it will be years before I can recover myself; and as to being fit for service, it is out of the question. I am therefore going to my brother-in-law at Melbourne. The ship sails tomorrow. Perhaps the long voyage may set me up. I do nothing now but start and tremble, and fancy IT is behind me. I humbly beg you, honoured sir, to order my clothes, and whatever wages are due to me, to be sent to my mother's, at Walworth — John knows her address.'

The letter ended with additional apologies, somewhat incoherent, and explanatory details as to effects that had been under the writer's charge.

This flight may perhaps warrant a suspicion that the man wished to go to Australia, and had been somehow or other fraudulently mixed up with the events of the night. I say nothing in refutation of that conjecture; rather, I suggest it as one that would seem to many persons the most probable solution of improbable occurrences. My belief in my own theory remained unshaken. I returned in the evening to the house, to bring away in a hackcab the things I had left there, with my poor dog's body. In this task I was not disturbed, nor did any incident worth note befall me, except that still, on ascending and descending the stairs, I heard the same footfall in advance. On leaving the house, I went to Mr J--'s. He was at home. I returned him the keys, told him that my curiosity was sufficiently gratified, and was about to relate quickly what had passed, when he stopped me, and said, though with much politeness, that he had no longer any interest in a mystery which none had ever solved.

I determined at least to tell him of the two letters I had read, as well as of the extraordinary manner in which they had disappeared, and I then inquired if he thought they had been addressed to the woman who had died in the house, and if there were anything in her early history which could possibly confirm the dark suspicions to which the letters gave rise. Mr J-- seemed startled, and after musing a few moments, answered, 'I am but little acquainted with the woman's earlier history, except, as I before told you, that her family were known to mine. But you revive some vague reminiscences to her prejudice. I will make inquiries, and inform you of their result. Still, even if we could admit the popular superstition that a person who had been either the perpetrator or the victim of dark crimes in life could revisit, as a restless spirit, the scene in which those crimes had been committed, I should observe that the house was infested by strange sights and sounds before the old woman died — you smile — what would you say?'

'I would say this, that I am convinced, if we could get to the bottom of these mysteries, we should find a living human agency.'

'What! you believe it is all an imposture? for what object?'

'Not an imposture in the ordinary sense of the word. If suddenly I were to sink into a deep sleep, from which you could not awake me, but in that sleep could answer questions with an accuracy which I could not pretend to when awake — tell you what money you had in your pocket — nay, describe your very thoughts — it is not necessarily an imposture, any more than it is necessarily supernatural. I should be, unconsciously to myself, under a mesmeric influence, conveyed to me from a distance by a human being who had acquired power over me by previous *rapport.*'

'But if a mesmerizer could so affect another living being, can you suppose that a mesmerizer could so affect inanimate objects; move chairs — open and shut doors?'

'Or impress our senses with the belief in such effects — we never having been *en rapport* with the person acting on us? No. What is commonly called mesmerism could not do this; but there may be a power akin to mesmerism, and superior to it — the power that in the old days was called Magic. That such a power may extend to all inanimate objects of matter, I do not say; but if so, it would not be against nature — it would be only a rare power in nature which might be given to constitutions with certain peculiarities, and cultivated by practice to an extraordinary degree. That such a power might extend over the dead — that is, over certain thoughts and memories that the dead may still retain — and compel, not that which ought properly to be called the SOUL, and which is far beyond human reach, but rather a phantom of what has been most earth-stained on earth, to make itself apparent to our senses — is a very ancient though obsolete theory, upon which I will hazard no opinion. But I do not conceive the power would be supernatural. Let me illustrate what I mean from an experiment which Paracelsus describes as not difficult, and which the author of the *Curiosities of Literature* cites as credible: — A flower perishes; you burn it. Whatever were the elements of that flower while it lived are gone, dispersed, you know not whither; you can never discover nor re-collect them. But you can, by chemistry, out of the burnt dust of that flower, raise a spectrum of the flower, just as it seemed in life. It may be the same with the human being. The soul has as much escaped you as the essence or elements of the flower. Still you may make a spectrum of it. And this phantom, though in the popular superstition it is held to be the soul of the departed, must not be confounded with the true soul; it is but the image of the dead form. Hence, like the best-attested stories of ghosts or spirits, the thing that most strikes us is the absence of what we held to be soul; that is, of superior emancipated intelligence. These apparitions come for little or no object — they seldom speak when they do come; if they speak, they utter no idea above those of an ordinary person on earth. American spirit-seers have published volumes of communications in prose and verse, which they assert to be given in the names of the most illustrious dead — Shakespeare, Bacon — heaven knows whom. Those communications, taking the best, are certainly not a whit of higher order than would be communications from living persons of fair talent and educa- tion; they are wondrously inferior to what Bacon, Shakespeare, and Plato said and wrote when on earth. Nor, what is more noticeable, do they ever contain an idea that was not on the earth before. Wonderful, therefore, as such phenomena may be (granting them to be truthful), I see much that philosophy may question, nothing that it is incumbent on philosophy to deny — viz., nothing supernatural. They are but ideas conveyed somehow or other (we have not yet discovered the means) from one mortal brain to another. Whether, in so doing, tables walk of their own accord, or fiend-like shapes appear in a magic circle, or bodyless hands rise and remove material objects, or a Thing of Darkness, such as presented itself to me, freeze our blood — still I am persuaded that these are but agencies conveyed, as by electric wires, to my own brain from the brain of another. In some

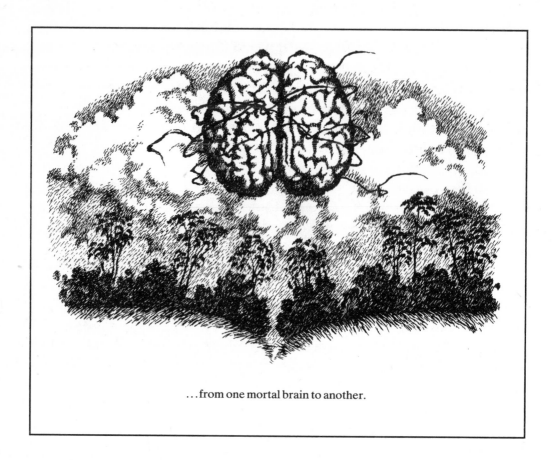

...from one mortal brain to another.

constitutions there is a natural chemistry, and those constitutions may produce chemic wonders — in others a natural fluid, call it electricity, and these may produce electric wonders. But the wonders differ from Normal Science in this — they are alike objectless, purposeless, puerile, frivolous. They lead on to no grand results; and therefore the world does not heed, and true sages have not cultivated them. But sure I am, that of all I saw or heard, a man, human as myself, was the remote originator; and I believe unconsciously to himself as to the exact effects produced, for this reason: no two persons, you say, have ever told you that they experienced exactly the same thing. Well, observe, no two persons ever experience exactly the same dream. If this were an ordinary imposture, the machinery would be arranged for results that would but little vary; if it were a supernatural agency permitted by the Almighty, it would surely be for some definite end. These phenomena belong to neither class; my persuasion is, that they originate in some brain now far distant; that that brain had no distinct volition in anything that occurred; that what does occur reflects but its devious, motley, ever-shifting, half-formed thoughts; in short, that it has been but the dreams of such a brain put into action and invested with a semi-substance. That this brain is of immense power, that it can set matter into movement, that it is malignant and destructive, I believe; some material force must have killed my dog; the same force might, for aught I know, have sufficed to kill myself, had I been as subjugated by terror as that dog – had my intellect or my spirit given me no countervailing resistance in my will.'

'It killed your dog! that is fearful! indeed it is strange that no animal can be induced to stay in that house; not even a cat. Rats and mice are never found in it.'

'The instincts of the brute creation detect influences deadly to their existence. Man's reason has a sense less subtle, because it has a resisting power more supreme. But enough; do you comprehend my theory?'

'Yes, though imperfectly – and I except my crotchet (pardon the word), however odd, rather than embrace at once the notions of ghosts and hobgoblins we imbibed in our nurseries. Still, to my unfortunate house the evil is the same. What on earth can I do with the house?'

'I will tell you what I would do. I am convinced from my own internal feelings that the small unfurnished room at right angles to the door of the bedroom which I occupied, forms a starting-point or receptacle for the influences which haunt the house; and I strongly advise you to have the walls opened, the floor removed – nay, the whole room pulled down. I observe that it is detached from the body of the house, built over the small back-yard, and could be removed without injury to the rest of the building.'

'And you think, if I did that--'

'You would cut off the telegraph wires. Try it. I am so persuaded that I am right, that I will pay half the expense if you will allow me to direct the operations.'

'Nay, I am well able to afford the cost; for the rest, allow me to write to you.'

About ten days afterward I received a letter from Mr J--, telling me that he had visited the house since I had seen him; that he had found the two letters I had described, replaced in the drawer from which I had taken them; that he had read them with misgivings like my own; that he had instituted a cautious inquiry about the woman to whom I rightly conjectured they had been written. It seemed that thirty-six years ago (a year before the date of the letters) she had married, against the wish of her relations, an American of very suspicious character; in fact, he was generally believed to have been a pirate. She herself was the daughter of very respectable tradespeople, and had served in the capacity of a nursery governess before her marriage. She had a brother, a widower, who was considered wealthy, and who had one child of about six years old. A month after the marriage, the body of this brother was found in the Thames, near London Bridge; there seemed some marks of violence about his throat, but they were not deemed sufficient to warrant the inquest in any other verdict than that of 'found drowned'.

The American and his wife took charge of the little boy, the deceased brother having by his will left his sister guardian of his only child — and in event of the child's death, the sister inherited. The child died about six months afterward — it was supposed to have been neglected and ill-treated. The neighbours deposed to have heard it shriek at night. The surgeon who had examined it after death, said that it was emaciated as if from the want of nourishment, and the body was covered with livid bruises. It seemed that one winter night the child had sought to escape — crept out into the back-yard — tried to scale the wall — fallen back exhausted, and been found at morning on the stones in a dying state. But though there was some evidence of cruelty, there was none of murder: and the aunt and her husband had sought to palliate cruelty by alleging the exceeding stubbornness and perversity of the child, who was declared to be half-witted. Be that as it may, at the orphan's death the aunt inherited her brother's fortune. Before the first wedded year was out, the American had quitted England abruptly, and never returned to it. He obtained a cruising vessel, which was lost in the Atlantic two years afterwards. The widow was left in affluence; but reverses of various kinds had befallen her; a bank broke — an investment failed — she went into a small business and became insolvent — then she entered into service, sinking lower and lower, from house-keeper down to maid-of-all-work — never long retaining a place, though nothing decided against her character was ever alleged. She was considered sober, honest, and peculiarly quiet in her ways; still nothing prospered with her. And so she had dropped into the work-house, from which Mr J-- had taken her, to be placed in charge of the very house which she had rented as mistress in the first year of her wedded life.

Mr J-- added that he had passed an hour alone in the unfurnished room which I had urged him to destroy, and that his impressions of dread while there were so great, though he had neither heard nor seen anything, that he was eager to have the walls bared and the floors removed as I had suggested. He had engaged persons for the work, and would commence any day I would name.

The day was accordingly fixed. I repaired to the haunted house — we went into the blind, dreary room, took up the skirting, and then the floors. Under the rafters, covered with rubbish, was found a trap-door, quite large enough to admit a man. It was closely nailed down, with clamps and rivets of iron. On removing these we descended into a room below, the existence of which had never been suspected. In this room there had been a window and a flue, but they had been bricked over, evidently for many years. By the help of candles we examined this place; it still retained some mouldering furniture — three chairs, an oak settle, a table — all of the fashion of about eighty years ago. There was a chest of drawers against the wall, in which we found, half-rotted away, old-fashioned articles of a man's dress, such as might have been worn eighty or a hundred years ago by a gentleman of some rank — costly steel buckles and buttons, like those yet worn in court-dresses — a handsome court-sword — in a waist-coat which had once been rich with goldlace, but which was now blackened and foul with damp, we found five guineas, a few silver coins, and an ivory ticket, probably for some place of entertainment long since passed away. But our main discovery was in a kind of iron safe fixed to the wall, the lock of which it cost us much trouble to get picked.

In this safe were three shelves, and two small drawers. Ranged on the shelves were several small bottles of crystal hermetically stopped. They contained colourless volatile essences, of the nature of which I shall only say that they were not poisons — phosphor and ammonia entered into some of them. There were also some very curious glass tubes, and a small pointed rod of iron, with a large lump of rock-crystal, and another of amber — also a loadstone of great power.

In one of the drawers we found a miniature portrait set in gold, and retaining the freshness of its colours most remarkably, considering the length of time it had probably been there. The portrait was that of a man who might be somewhat advanced in middle life, perhaps forty-seven or forty-eight.

It was a remarkable face — a most impressive face. If you could fancy some mighty serpent transformed into man, preserving in the human lineaments the old serpent type, you would have a better idea of that countenance than long descriptions can convey; the width and flatness of frontal — the tapering elegance of contour disguising the strength of the deadly jaw — the long, large, terrible eye, glittering and green as the emerald — and withal a certain ruthless calm, as if from the consciousness of an immense power.

Mechanically I turned round the miniature to examine the back of it, and on the back was engraved a pentacle; in the middle of the pentacle a ladder, and the third step of the ladder was formed by the date of 1765. Examining still more minutely, I detected a spring; this, on being pressed, opened the back of the miniature as a lid. Within-side the lid was engraved, 'Mariana, to thee-- Be faithful in life and in death to--.' Here follows a name that I will not mention, but it was not unfamiliar to me. I had heard it spoken of by old men in my childhood as the name borne by a dazzling charlatan who had made a great sensation in London for a year or so, and had fled the country on the charge of a double murder within his own house — that of his mistress and his rival. I said nothing of this to Mr J--, to whom reluctantly, I resigned the miniature.

We had found no difficulty in opening the first drawer within the iron safe; we found great difficulty in opening the second; it was not locked, but it resisted all efforts, till we inserted in the chinks the edge of a chisel. When we had thus drawn it forth, we found a very singular apparatus in the nicest order. Upon a small, thin book, or rather tablet, was placed a saucer of crystal; this saucer was filled with a clear liquid — on that liquid floated a kind of compass, with a needle shifting rapidly round; but instead of the usual points of a compass were seven strange characters, not very unlike those used by astrologers to denote the planets. A peculiar, but not strong nor displeasing odour, came from this drawer, which was lined with a wood that we afterwards discovered to be hazel. Whatever the cause of this odour, it produced a material effect on the nerves. We all felt it, even the two workmen who were in the room — a creeping, tingling sensation from the tip of the fingers to the roots of the hair. Impatient to examine the tablet

I removed the saucer. As I did so the needle of the compass went round and round with exceeding swiftness, and I felt a shock that ran through my whole frame, so that I dropped the saucer on the floor. The liquid was spilt — the saucer was broken — the compass rolled to the other end of the room — and at that instant the walls shook to and fro, as if a giant had swayed and rocked them.

The two workmen were so frightened that they ran up the ladder by which they had descended from the trap-door; but seeing that nothing more happened, they were easily induced to return.

Meanwhile I had opened the tablet; it was bound in plain red leather, with a silver clasp; it contained but one sheet of thick vellum, and on that sheet were inscribed, within a double pentacle, words in old monkish Latin, which are literally to be translated thus: — 'On all that it can reach within these walls — sentient or inanimate, living or dead — as moves the needle, so work my will! Accursed be the house, and restless be the house, and restless be the dwellers therein.'

We found no more. Mr J-- burnt the tablet and its anathema. He razed to the foundations the part of the building containing the secret room with the chamber over it. He had then the courage to inhabit the house himself for a month, and a quieter, better-conditioned house could not be found in all London. Subsequently he let it to advantage, and his tenant has made no complaints.

But my story is not yet done. A few days after Mr J-- had removed into the house, I paid him a visit. We were standing by the open window and conversing. A van containing some articles of furniture which he was moving from his former house was at the door.

I had just urged on him my theory that all those phenomena regarded as supermundane had emanated from a human brain; adducing the charm, or rather curse we had found and destroyed, in support of my theory.

Mr J-- was observing in reply, 'that even if mesmerism, or whatever analogous power it might be called, could really thus work in the absence of the operator, and produce effects so extraordinary, still could those effects continue when the operator himself was dead? and if the spell had been wrought, and, indeed, the room walled up, more than seventy years ago, the probability was that the operator had long since departed this life' — Mr J--, I say, was thus answering, when I caught hold of his arm and pointed to the street below.

A well-dressed man had crossed from the opposite side, and was accosting the carrier in charge of the van. His face, as he stood, was exactly fronting our window. It was the face of the miniature we had discovered; it was the face of the portrait of the noble three centuries ago.

'Good heavens!' cried Mr J--, 'that is the face of De V--, and scarcely a day older than when I saw it in the Rajah's court in my youth!'

Seized by the same thought, we both hastened downstairs; I was first in the street, but the man had already gone. I caught sight of him, however, not many yards in advance, and in another moment I was by his side.

I had resolved to speak to him, but when I looked into his face I felt as if it were impossible to do so. That eye — the eye of the serpent — fixed and held me spellbound. And withal, about the man's whole person there was a dignity, an air of pride and station and superiority that would have made anyone, habituated to the usages of the world, hesitate long before venturing upon a liberty or impertinence.

And what could I say? What was it I could ask?

Thus ashamed of my first impulse, I fell a few paces back, still, however, following the stranger, undecided what else to do. Meanwhile he turned the corner of the street; a plain carriage was in waiting with a servant out of livery, dressed like a *valet de place,* at the carriage door. In another moment he had stepped into the carriage, and it drove off. I returned to the house.

Mr J-- was still at the street door. He had asked the carrier what the stranger had said to him.

'Merely asked whom that house now belonged to.'

The same evening I happened to go with a friend to a place in town called the Cosmopolitan Club, a place open to men of all countries, all opinions, all degrees. One orders one's coffee, smokes one's cigar. One is always sure to meet agreeable, sometimes remarkable persons.

I had not been two minutes in the room before I beheld at table, conversing with an acquaintance of mine, whom I will designate by the initial G--, the man, the original of the miniature. He was now without his hat, and the likeness was yet more startling, only I observed that while he was conversing, there was less severity in the countenance; there was even a smile, though a very quiet and very cold one. The dignity of mien I had acknowledged in the street was also more striking; a dignity akin to that which invests some prince of the East, conveying the idea of supreme indifference and habitual, indisputable, indolent but resistless power.

G-- soon after left the stranger, who then took up a scientific journal, which seemed to absorb his attention.

I drew G-- aside.

'Who and what is that gentleman?'

'That? Oh, a very remarkable man indeed! I met him last year amid the caves of Petra, the Scriptural Edom. He is the best Oriental scholar I know. We joined company, had an adventure with robbers, in which he showed

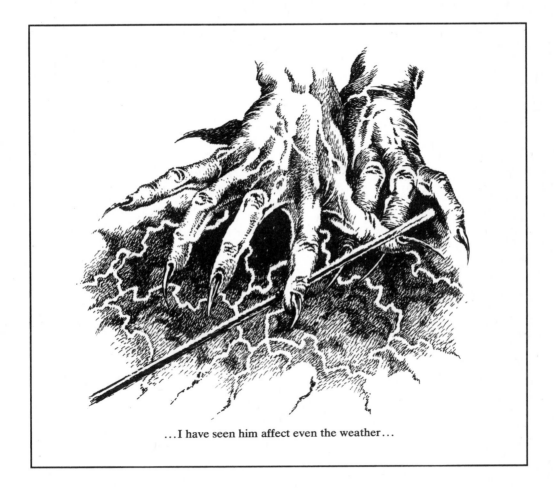

...I have seen him affect even the weather...

a coolness that saved our lives; afterwards he invited me to spend a day with him in a house he had bought at Damascus, buried among almond blossoms and roses — the most beautiful thing! He had lived there for some time, quite as an Oriental, in grand style.

'I half suspect he is a renegade, immensely rich, very odd; by the by, a great mesmerizer. I have seen him with my own eyes produce an effect on inanimate things. If you take a letter from your pocket and throw it to the other end of the room, he will order it to come to his feet, and you will see the letter wriggle itself along the floor till it has obeyed his command. 'Pon my honour 'tis true; I have seen him affect even the weather, disperse or collect clouds by means of a glass tube or wand. But he does not like talking of these matters to strangers. He has only just arrived in England; says he has not been here for a great many years; let me introduce him to you.'

'Certainly! He is English, then? What is his name?'

'Oh! a very homely one – Richards.'

'And what is his birth – his family?'

'How do I know? What does it signify? No doubt some *parvenu;* but rich, so infernally rich!'

G-- drew me up to the stranger, and the introduction was effected. The manners of Mr Richards were not those of an adventurous traveller. Travellers are in general gifted with high animal spirits; they are talkative, eager, imperious. Mr Richards was calm and subdued in tone, with manners which were made distant by the loftiness of punctilious courtesy, the manners of a former age.

I observed that the English he spoke was not exactly of our day. I should even have said that the accent was slightly foreign. But then Mr Richards remarked that he had been little in the habit for years of speaking in his native tongue.

The conversation fell upon the changes in the aspects of London since he had last visited our metropolis. G-- then glanced off to the moral changes – literary, social, political – the great men who were removed from the stage within the last twenty years; the new great men who were coming on.

In all this Mr Richards evinced no interest. He had evidently read none of our living authors, and seemed scarcely acquainted by name with our younger statesmen. Once, and only once, he laughed; it was when G-- asked him whether he had any thoughts of getting into Parliament; and the laugh was inward, sarcastic, sinister – a sneer raised into a laugh.

After a few minutes, G-- left us to talk to some other acquaintances who had just lounged into the room, and I then said, quietly:

'I have seen a miniature of you, Mr Richards, in the house you once inhabited, and perhaps built – if not wholly, at least in part – in Oxford Street. You passed by that house this morning.'

Not till I had finished did I raise my eyes to his, and then he fixed my gaze so steadfastly that I could not withdraw it — those fascinating serpent-eyes. But involuntarily, and as if the words that translated my thoughts were dragged from me, I added, in a low whisper, 'I have been a student in the mysteries of life and nature; of those mysteries I have known the occult professors. I have the right to speak to you thus.' And I uttered a certain password.

'Well, I concede the right. What would you ask?'

'To what extent human will in certain temperaments can extend?'

'To what extent can thought extend? Think, and before you draw breath you are in China!'

'True; but my thought has no power in China.'

'Give it expression, and it may have. You may write down a thought which, sooner or later, may alter the whole condition of China. What is a law but a thought? Therefore thought is infinite. Therefore thought has power; no in proportion to its value — a bad thought may make a bad law as potent as a good thought can make a good one.'

'Yes, what you say confirms my own theory. Through invisible currents one human brain may transmit its ideas to other human brains, with the same rapidity as a thought promulgated by visible means. And as thought is imperishable, as it leaves its stamp behind it in the natural world, even when the thinker has passed out of this world, so the thought of the living may have power to rouse up and revive the thoughts of the dead, such as those thoughts *were in life,* though the thought of the living cannot reach the thoughts which the dead *now* may entertain. Is it not so?'

'I decline to answer, if in my judgment thought has the limit you would fix to it. But proceed, you have a special question you wish to put.'

'Intense malignity is an intense will, engendered in a peculiar temperament, and aided by natural means within the reach of science, may produce effects like those ascribed of old to evil magic. It might thus haunt the walls of a human habitation with spectral revivals of all guilty thoughts and guilty deeds once conceived and done within those walls; all, in short, with which the evil will claims *rapport* and affinity — imperfect, incoherent, fragmentary snatches at the old dramas acted therein years ago.

'Thoughts thus crossing each other haphazard, as in the nightmare of a vision, growing up into phantom sights and sounds, and all serving to create horror; not because those sights and sounds are really visitations from a world without, but that they are ghastly, monstrous renewals of what have been in this world itself, set into malignant play by a malignant mortal.

And it is through the material agency of that human brain that these things would acquire even a human power; would strike as with the shock of electricity, and might kill, if the thought of the person assailed did not rise superior to the dignity of the original assailer; might kill the most powerful animal, if unnerved by fear, but not injure the feeblest man, if, while his flesh crept, his mind stood out fearless.

'Thus when in old stories we read of a magician rent to pieces by the fiends he had invoked, or still more, in Eastern legends, that one magician succeeds by arts in destroying another, there may be so far truth, that a material being has clothed, from his own evil propensities, certain elements and fluids, usually quiescent or harmless, with awful shapes and terrific force; just as the lightning, that has lain hidden and innocent in the cloud, becomes by natural law suddenly visible, takes a distinct shape to the eye, and can strike destruction on the object to which it is attracted.'

'You are not without glimpses of a mighty secret,' said Mr Richards composedly. 'According to your view, could the mortal obtain the power you speak of, he would necessarily be a malignant and evil being.'

'If the power were exercised as I have said, most malignant and most evil; though I believe in the ancient traditions that he could not injure the good. His will could only injure those with whom it has established an affinity, or over whom it forces unresisted sway. I will now imagine an example that may be within the laws of nature, yet seem wild as the fables of a bewildered monk.

'You will remember that Albertus Magnus, after describing minutely the process by which the spirits may be invoked and commanded, adds emphatically that the process will instruct and avail only to the few; that *a man must be born a magician!* — that is, born with a peculiar physical temperament, as a man is born a poet.

'Rarely are men in whose constitutions lurks this occult power of the highest order of intellect; usually in the intellect there is some twist, perversity, or disease. But on the other hand, they must possess, to an astonishing degree, the faculty to concentrate thought on a single object — the energic faculty that we call WILL. Therefore, though their intellect be not sound, it is exceedingly forcible for the attainment of what it desires. I will imagine such a person, pre-eminently gifted with this constitution and its concomitant forces. I will place him in the loftier grades of society.

'I will suppose his desires emphatically those of the sensualist; he has, therefore, a strong love of life. He is an absolute egotist; his will is concentred in himself; he has fierce passions; he knows no enduring, no holy affections, but he can covet eagerly what for the moment he desires; he can hate implacably what opposes itself to his objects; he can commit fearful crimes, yet feel small remorse; he resorts rather to curses upon others than to penitence for his misdeeds. Circumstances to which his constitution guides him, lead him to a rare knowledge of the natural secrets which may serve his egotism. He is a close observer where his passions encourage observation; he is a minute calculator, not from love of truth, but where love of self sharpens his faculties; therefore he can be a man of science.

'I suppose such a being, having by experience learned the power of his arts over others, trying what may be the power of will over his own frame, and studying all that in natural philosophy may increase that power. He loves life, he dreads death; *he wills to live on.* He cannot restore himself to youth; he cannot entirely stay the progress of death; he cannot make himself immortal in the flesh and blood. But he may arrest, for a time so long as to appear incredible if I said it, that hardening of the parts which constitutes old age.

'A year may age him no more than an hour ages another. His intense will, scientifically trained into system, operates in short, over the wear and tear of his own frame. He lives on. That he may not seem a portent and miracle, he *dies,* from time to time, seemingly, to certain persons. Having schemed the transfer of a wealth that suffices to his wants, he disappears from one corner of the world, and contrives that his obsequies shall be celebrated.

'He reappears at another corner of the world, where he resides undetected, and does not visit the scenes of his former career till all who could remember his features are no more. He would be profoundly miserable if he had affections; he has none but for himself. No good man would accept his longevity; and to no man, good or bad, would he or could he communicate its true secret.

'Such a man may exist; such a man as I have described I see now before me — Duke of --, in the court of --, dividing time between lust and brawl, alchemists and wizards; again, in the last century, charlatan and criminal, with name less noble, domiciled in the house at which you gazed to-day, and flying from the law you had outraged, none knew whither; traveller once more revisiting London with the same earthly passion which filled your heart when races now no more walked through yonder streets; outlaw from the school of all the noble and diviner mysteries. Execrable image of life in death and death in life, I warn you back from the cities and homes of healthful men! back to the ruins of departed empires! back to the deserts of nature unredeemed!'

There answered me a whisper so musical, so potently musical, that it seemed to enter into my whole being and subdue me despite myself. Thus it said:

'I have sought one like you for the last hundred years. Now I have found you, we part not till I know what I desire. The vision that sees through the past and cleaves through the veil of the future is in you at this hour − never before, never to come again. The vision of no pulling, fantastic girl, of no sick-bed somnambule, but of a strong man with a vigorous brain. Soar, and look forth!'

As he spoke, I felt as if I rose out of myself upon eagle wings. All the weight seemed gone from air, roofless the room, roofless the dome of space. I was not in the body − where, I knew not; but aloft over time, over earth.

Again I heard the melodious whisper:

'You say right. I have mastered great secrets by the power of will. True, by will and by science I can retard the process of years, but death comes not by age alone. Can I frustrate the accidents which bring death upon the young?'

'No; every accident is a providence. Before a providence snaps every human will.'

'Shall I die at last, ages and ages hence, by the slow though inevitable growth of time, or by the cause that I call accident?'

'By a cause you call accident.'

'Is not the end still remote?' asked the whisper, with a slight tremor.

'Regarded as my life regards time, it is still remote.'

'And shall I, before then, mix with the world of men as I did ere I learned these secrets; resume eager interest in their strife and their trouble; battle with ambition, and use the power of the sage to win the power that belongs to kings?'

'You will yet play a part on the earth that will fill earth with commotion and amaze. For wondrous designs have you, a wonder yourself, been permitted to live on through the centuries. All the secrets you have stored will then have their uses; all that now makes you a stranger amid the generations will contribute then to make you their lord. As the trees and the straws are drawn into a whirlpool, as they spin round, are sucked to the deep, and again tossed aloft by the eddies, so shall races and thrones be drawn into your vortex. Awful destroyer! but in destroying, made, against your own will, a constructor.'

'And the date, too, is far off?'

'Far off; when it comes, think your end in this world is at hand!'

'How and what is the end? Look east, west, south, and north.'

'In the north, where you never yet trod, towards the point whence your instincts have warned you, there a spectre will seize you. 'Tis Death! I see a ship; it is haunted; 'tis chased! it sails on. Baffled navies sail after that ship. It enters the region of ice. It passes a sky red with meteors. Two moons stand on high, over ice-reefs. I see the ship locked between white defiles; they are ice-rocks. I see the dead strew the decks, stark and livid, green mould on their limbs. All are dead but one man — it is you! But years, though so slowly they come, have then scathed you. There is the coming of age on your brow, and the will is relaxed in the cells of the brain. Still that will, though enfeebled, exceeds all that man knew before you; through the will you live on, gnawed with famine. And Nature no longer obeys you in that death-spreading region; the sky is a sky of iron, and the air has iron clamps, and the ice-rocks wedge in the ship. Hark how it cracks and groans! Ice will imbed it as amber imbeds a straw. And a man has gone forth, living yet, from the ship and its dead; and he has clambered up the spikes of an iceberg, and the two moons gaze down on his form. That man is yourself, and terror is on you — terror; and terror has swallowed up your will.

'And I see, swarming up the steep ice-rock, grey, grizzly things. The bears of the North have scented their quarry; they come nearer and nearer, shambling, and rolling their bulk. In that day every moment shall seem to you longer than the centuries which you have passed. Heed this: after life, moments continued make the bliss or the hell of eternity.'

'Hush!' said the whisper. 'But the day, you assure me, is far off, very far! I go back to the almond and rose of Damascus! Sleep!'

The room swam before my eyes I became insensible. When I recovered, I found G-- holding my hand and smiling. He said, 'You, who have always declared yourself proof against mesmerism, have succumbed at last to my friend Richards.'

'Where is Mr Richards?'

'Gone when you passed into a trance, saying quietly to me, 'Your friend will not wake for an hour.'

I asked, as collectedly as I could, where Mr Richards lodged.

'At the Trafalgar Hotel.'

'Give me your arm,' said I to G--. 'Let us call on him; I have something to say.'

When we arrived to the hotel we were told that Mr Richards had returned twenty minutes before, paid his bill, left directions with his servant (a Greek) to pack his effect, and proceed to Malta by the steamer that should leave Southampton the next day. Mr Richards had merely said of his own movements that he had visits to pay in the neighbourhood of London, and it was uncertain whether he should be able to reach Southampton in time for that steamer; if not, he should follow in the next one.

The waiter asked me my name. On my informing him, he gave me a note that Mr Richards had left for me in case I called.

The note was as follows:

I wished you to utter what was in your mind. You obeyed. I have therefore established power over you. For three months from this day you can communicate to no living man what has passed between us. You cannot even show this note to the friend by your side. During three months silence complete as to me and mine. Do you doubt my power to lay on you this command? Try to disobey me. At the end of the third month the spell is raised. For the rest, I spare you. I shall visit your grave a year and a day after it has received you.

So ends the strange story, which I ask no one to believe. I write it down exactly three months after I received the above note. I could not write it before, nor could I show to G--, in spite of his urgent request, the note which I read under the gas lamp by his side.

E. Bulwer-Lytton